A King's Gambit

Wind of Destiny, Volume Two

AJ Cooper

A King's Gambit
Copyright © 2016 Andrew James Cooper
Published by Realms of Varda
www.vardabooks.com

All Rights Reserved. No part of this book may be reproduced, scanned, or distributed in any print or electronic form without permission.

All characters appearing in this work are fictitious. Any resemblance to real persons, living or dead, is purely coincidental.

Front cover art © Breakermaximus | Dreamstime.com

Back cover art © Desislava Vasileva | Dreamstime.com

ISBN 978-1-958724-01-9

SANCTON
THE BLESSED ISLES
Eloesus
RIVER SULIS
PALLISTRIX
ISTEROS
ARCTOS
100 mi.
200 mi.
300 mi.
400 mi.
500 mi.
AGATHÉ
TIGRIS
IOGHEIRA
STRAITEIRA
THÉNAI
THENOA
KERSEPOLI
KERSICA
KORTHOS
KORTHICA
TEN CITIES
THARTA
THARTICA
ARKADIOS
THEMURIA

THE TRIUMPHAL ENTRY

The gates to the city swung open and loud drumming began. Citizens of Tharta—rich and poor alike—had crowded the main thoroughfare to glimpse their newest queen. The procession began with turbaned dancers in billowing white pants, tossing torches from one hand to the other and then between themselves—thirty in all—a people from a far-off land who had never been seen in Eloesus before.

What came next, the Thartans could scarcely believe—gray-skinned beasts larger than any animal in Eloesus, with a swaying trunk for a nose. The legendary "elephants" had come, painted red and white in war paint and controlled by turbaned mahouts. There were loud shouts among the lookers-on, startled gasps by Tharta's citizenry. Little children clapped excitedly; mothers grabbed them close to keep them from the danger.

After the elephants came horse-drawn chariots, painted red, green and orange in hues that seemed to glow like fire. The wheels of the chariots were inset with rubies and diamonds. The Thartans had never seen such wealth before. Even the drivers were richly dressed: a dozen in all, wearing conical hats encrusted with diamonds and long purple robes gleaming with rubies, fire opals and sapphires.

Next came a giant chariot pulled by oxen. It was flanked by copper-skinned Khazidees, who began tossing coins freely into the crowd. The people fell over themselves to stuff their pockets with the gold and silver. At the sight of the chaos, another man on the chariot—half again as tall as the Khazidees—let out a belly laugh. The learned in the crowd knew him as Khusruh, the Vizier of Fharas, a eunuch from the empire's nether regions and the highest-ranked in the King of Kings' court. He, too, was richly dressed—a gown of Khazidean purple, silken with gold trim, and a great jagged crown of gold inset with fiery rubies and verdant emeralds. A single gem in his crown was as much wealth as any in the crowd would see in their lifetime.

Next came a giant brazier pulled by a dozen horses. A giant fire was burning within; this represented the Fharese god. The people of the Far South did not craft images of their gods like the Eloesians. The bright burning fire, it seemed, was enough.

The crowd could scarcely imagine the newest queen's beauty. Her name was Zubeida—in the tongue of Fharas, "water lily."

A parade of caged white tigers came next, trapped in iron bars and yet snarling and eager to get out, clawing at the terrified yet mesmerized crowd. Next came the drummers, brawny ponytailed men in leathers, the source of the music. Two trumpets blew, and a litter appeared. The crowd held their breath as the princess was lifted high—and gasped in confusion. The princess was covered, head to toe, in black, with no part of her face or body showing. It seemed they would never behold Tharta's newest queen.

~

A familiar panic rose up in Gygax's stomach as he saw Zubeida. She had covered herself completely; Gygax could see her from the palace balcony, and yet not through that thick woolen garb. Had he made a mistake? Why would she cover herself? Was she terribly ugly?

It did not matter. This whole marriage was political; it had no basis in love. With Zubeida as his wife, the city of Tharta and the Fharese Empire would be pulled closer. Tharta would never have to fear again. Gygax's father had begun the process of what he called "Fharaizing." He had deepened trade links with the empire and forced many city officials to divorce their wives, then marry Fharese women. He had built shrines to the fire god Athra and hosted officials from Fharas regularly. The relationship had been strengthened by the older Gygax; now, with this marriage, it would be permanent. The City of Tharta would become indelibly etched into the fabric of Fharas.

But that didn't mean Gygax wasn't nervous, or that he didn't want to hide in the palace garden. He could not help but wonder if he was making a mistake. Tharta made great boasts of its cosmopolitan nature, of its great wealth and openness of mind. But Fharas was alien, was it not? It was autocratic, ruled by a single leader without any form of council or democracy. Did Gygax truly understand what was at stake?

I have already made my decision. There was no going back, now.

Gygax met the Fharese party in the palace yard. There, Khusruh met him—the eunuch whose power in the world was unmatched save for the King of Kings himself. *The vizier.* Should Gygax fall prostrate? Zubeida was nowhere to be seen.

"Forgive me," boomed Khusruh. "Zubeida is with her handmaids. She will not come near you until the wedding night."

"And she has covered herself—" Gygax started.

"Zubeida is a Shakrathite," Khusruh said. "Fharese women only need cover their hair when they are married; but in Shakrath they view any portion of the female body to be too enticing. All women are covered completely, both married and virgin."

"I see." The conversation had not stemmed Gygax's worries. Still, his stomach was twisting to knots.

"Zubeida is beautiful, though," Khusruh said. "She lives up to her name—a precious lily. You are a lucky man, Gygax."

"Am I," Gygax breathed. It did not feel like it, though he was the King of Tharta, the greatest city in Eloesus.

"As a eunuch, I am trusted completely," Khusruh said. "I accompany the King of Kings' wives even into the women's quarters. There, even a Shakrathite may disrobe."

Gygax didn't know what to say. So many things had happened this day. So many things that scared him. One thing was beyond all doubts—he had begun the transformation of Tharta and there was no going back.

Fharas and Tharta would be linked not through just trade or religion but by the most intimate of bonds—through blood.

TRUTH AND DECEPTION

Deep down within his fiery home
The dark lord Kronos burned with rage
He sent a viper out to kill
His foe, Phillipidēs the babe
Still wrapped in swaddling clothes was he
But when the viper meant to strike
He grabbed it with his tiny hands
And crushed its neck and flung it down
And awed the world and all who watched
Said "He is not born of a man—
A god's blood must run through his veins."

— Arkelaios

THE HOUSE OF THE ARCHON, THÉNAI

Theron awoke from his wounded stupor. He was covered in sweat and panting uncontrollably. The knife-wound blazed with pain as he sat up. The physician at his side forced him down.

"By the gods, you must rest!" he snapped. He lifted to Theron's mouth a canteen filled with foul-tasting medicine. He gulped it down anyway. Theron eyed the wounds and saw them covered in bandages and gauzes, with red having leaked through to the white. He had never felt so weak or so ill. He had never been so worried about his life. In his dazed and dizzy visions the shadows of the room had swirled around; surely grim Death was lurking just beyond the corner, waiting to drag him into hell. Soon he would be a shade floating through the underworld. Was such a grim and dreary existence better than this? He thought so. Perhaps the pain itself would kill him. But death would be a relief.

He recalled the news that had been brought to him—that the Thartan king Gygax had sent assassins his way. But why? Why would one Eloesian try to kill another? Were they not of one blood? Were they not of one bond? Were they not, in essence, one people?

The physician gently removed a bandage but Theron still screamed in pain. He rubbed the wound with some sort of salve and then laid on a clean bandage. "You have a harsh fever," he said. "You must take care not to scream. You must only relax."

Theron could not remember a time in his life he had been this miserable. *The thought of another hour, another minute, of this pain...*

Someone appeared before him, walking past the physician. He wore a chiton. Through Theron's daze and his swirling vision he recognized the face: Hyron, the chief of the People's Assembly. "Archon, I have news..."

"Not now," Theron tried to say but all that came out was a muffled gargle.

"There are reports…" Hyron seemed hesitant.

"Out with it," Theron tried to say but only gasped like a dying fish.

"The King of Kings has mobilized an army… an army such as no one has ever seen. A million strong. He intends to bring Eloesus into the imperial fold…"

Theron chose not to speak.

"The Assembly has voted—we will send a delegation to negotiate terms of surrender. You must approve our resolution… will you sign a writ?" Hyron asked.

"Leave him be!" snapped the physician. As always his mind was solely focused on the duty at hand—to bring Theron back from his grievous wounds.

Theron could not comprehend what Hyron said. The physician held him down tight. "Hush, hush," he whispered. "Hush."

Theron shut his eyes.

~

He dreamed of that day so many months ago, which seemed a lifetime away. He dreamed of Phaido standing in the theater, strumming his lyre and singing. He dreamed of Phaido's monologue, where he spoke of the Eloesians "perched, as it were, like frogs along a pond." The archon Epaphras had been so enraged by Phaido's speech against the King of Kings that it caused their exile.

At his name, the nations trembled: *King of Kings. Shahanshah. Padisha Emperor.* Did any human deserve such reverence? Was it not reserved for the gods alone?

At his name, the people bowed. At his name the earth seemed to quake. At his name it seemed even nature obeyed.

Theron watched as a river was drained away, revealing the mud and rock beneath. He watched as fertile fields were made desolate, as forests were razed for wood and piled into a burning pyre. He saw a man raised to the heavens, and untold millions lying prostrate at his name.

Who could stand against that name?

SEVEN LIONS THEATER, THARTA

"We Eloesians are funny creatures," said the actor, complementing his words with bold, pronounced gestures. "At an early age we left our home… we founded cities all across the seas. We are like frogs sitting around a pond… Surely our future will be bright, and we will make all lands into something like home."

Quartillo recognized the line about frogs and ponds—there were variations of it in many plays. This one, from the lesser known playwright Thilemon, was just one of many. Quartillo's friends in the Potters' District, the seediest part of Tharta, thought less of him because of his fascination with theater. He spent much of his money on plays—even here, in Seven Lions Theater, where the wealthy and the well-off attended. He had even begun to write one—though the most brutal torturer could never ply it out of him. If any of his friends found out he wrote plays, he'd be done for. The Mysterium would banish him from the order. No one took playwrights seriously, not anymore.

As was customary, attendees did not cheer or applaud. Here—or, at least, among the wealthy—it was considered the mark of a mob to do so. The other, lesser cities of Eloesus did so. Thartans were better. With quiet dignity they watched the play; with quiet dignity they left. They only discussed the play in the comfort and silence of their homes. Their two-*thalon* admission was praise enough.

Quartillo filed out with the rest of the audience. The claustrophobic theater fell away behind him. He passed by the lion statues—of which there were seven—and entered the open plaza where the theater had been built. Under the still-baking evening sun, few dallied outside. But there were people standing there, watching them. Strange people.

For one, they wore foreign garb. They did not wear chitons or even tunics; they were clothed in silken robes of flame orange, blue and red. They had bushy black beards—all save one, who stood taller than the others. He had an ebon complexion and dark eyes; he was clearly in his middle age, yet there was a youthful look to his face. On his head was a golden conical cap which was forged in tiers—the legendary apex of Fharese royalty. This was clearly a high ranking official.

Quartillo had watched as the Thartan royalty grew further and further from their Eloesian roots. The father of King Gygax had been a Fharaizer at heart; he had made a point of welcoming merchants of the Far South and even built small shrines to their gods to make them welcome. Now the current King Gygax had brought all his father's efforts to a fore; he had married into Fharese royalty. Tharta, and Eloesus, would never be the same.

This was clearly a group from the Fharese wedding party, lurking outside the theater. Were they searching for someone? One thing was certain; they did not care about him.

~

Quartillo took the winding road home. The grand plazas, mosaic squares, theaters, libraries and marble temples faded to worn brick roads and decaying buildings. Soon even the brick was gone, replaced with dirt and filth. The hovels and mudbrick buildings of the Potters' District appeared; the ever-present smoke of hearthfires hung thick, stinging the eyes, combined with the stench of human waste. The Thartans of the Royal Quarter took great pride in the cleanliness of their streets, cleaning filth and dirt as soon as it was made, but the folk of the Potters' District could not afford such luxuries. Here, survival was the chief goal of all.

Bread was hard to come by. Sometimes theft was the only option—even at a risk of a severed hand.

The sounds of the harp and voice greeted Quartillo as he turned down Nestor's Way. The familiar sign greeted him: "The Fattened Pig," it read, though few in the Potters' District could read. A painting of a pink pig helped the illiterate masses.

As soon as Quartillo entered the dingy mudbrick tavern a hand struck him on the back. The voice confirmed the identity. "Saw a play, did you?" asked Didyma. She was the highest ranking member of the Mysterium, outside the Master. It was strange that the gangly blonde-haired woman was such a skilled impersonator and a master lockpick. She had even taken on the personas of men before, and the well born of the Royal District had believed her. Didyma was, in short, the most valuable member of the Mysterium. That was why she ranked higher than Quartillo, though she was ineffably silly and made jests even when inappropriate.

"I'd rather not say," said Quartillo.

That was as good a confirmation as any to Didyma. She laughed. Some in the Mysterium thought his obsession with drama was a dreadful thing, bordering on a crime. Didyma only found humor in it. "About that," she said, "we must have a word in private."

Didyma called for a private room. Quartillo followed her through the tavern's aging mudbrick corridors before they came to a crumbling chamber, tucked away at some dead end. The tavernkeeper left them alone. The room smelled old and musty. There was dark mold growing on a cheap plaster wall. Almost all the plaster was gone, though, revealing the mudbrick face. The tavernkeeper perhaps did not have the time to remove it all, especially in this long-forgotten room.

Quartillo coughed. A glass of wine would have helped in this juncture, a great silver goblet. But most of the wine was hoarded by the folk of the Royal Quarter. Such a luxury would set Quartillo back two *doukon*.

Quartillo wondered again at Didyma's success as she set her lanky, awkward body down on a chair. He took his own seat across the table from her. How could such a person be so skilled, so good at what she did?

"The Fharese have begun to sink their teeth into the city," said Didyma, and her silly smile faded to a solemn frown. "There is talk of shutting down the theater, or at least certain plays."

"Why?" asked Quartillo. The theater was one of the oldest institutions in Eloesus; by law no topic was off limits. Not even the king escaped mockery. It was one way the people expressed themselves in a society that, by and large, did not tolerate dissent. Such an outcome would be tragic.

"The Fharese have no such traditions," said Didyma. "Our spies in the royal court said the vizier is concerned by the people gathering in large groups. He says it is a recipe for conspiracy and rebellion."

"Vizier," Quartillo repeated the foreign word. It did not roll easily off his tongue.

"The highest ranking official in Fharas except for the King of Kings himself," said Didyma. "He is here... he is consolidating the empire's grip over Tharta. The wedding is just one step, it is said. There is talk of building more temples to Fharese gods... even compelling the people to worship them."

"We have to stop it," said Quartillo. But what could they do? The Mysterium had no influence over the court. They had little direct influence over the people of Potters' District.

"The Master is watching it closely," said Didyma. "He has decided to send you on a mission... one of great importance to the

Mysterium."

But surely whatever mission the Master had in mind would be better orchestrated by Didyma. She ranked far higher than him and surely was an expert in everything demanded.

"The vizier has an immense stash of coins and jewels," said Didyma. "So much so that we could feed the people of the Potters' District for weeks."

"Surely the Master would send you," said Quartillo. "You are much better at it than me." He fell into a fit of coughing; the air was thick here, and poor in quality.

"The Master has taken a special interest in you," said Didyma. "He thinks you have great talent within, that you can be shaped—with requisite experience—into a great mimic."

Could he think of it as an actor in a play? Quartillo had—in his cramped, third-story room—acted out bits and pieces of his original play. It was something he did not want to admit.

"You have practiced much, no doubt," Didyma said.

Did she know?

"The art of mimcry, I mean…" Didyma apparently noticed the confusion on his face. "Now you will put your skills to the test. The mission is dangerous. You can still refuse."

"No," Quartillo answered. "I never back down from a challenge."

Didyma slid a piece of paper, cut into a rectangle, across the room. It was his mystery card, painted with a blue eye. He flipped it over and saw the role he would play.

THE PALACE COURTYARD, THARTA

Did the gods have a role in this, Quartillo wondered. The mystery card he had drawn had put him in the role of Echeron, the playwright. He had never put much stock in the gods but it seemed they were playing tricks on him, laughing at him from their high mountain sanctuaries. Echeron, a famous Thenoan playwright, had written a number of dramas, only some of which he had seen. It would take all the deceit and quick thinking Quartillo had to pull this role off.

A narrow corridor opened up into a grand courtyard of marble where green bushes and flowering plants grew. In the center was a bubbling fountain etched with reliefs of the ancient Megarine War: proud Thartans, nude and carrying only a shield for protection, fighting the Megarines—though Eloesian by blood, more southron in character. They were depicted wearing long robes and wielding wicker shields, with curved sabers in their hands. But back then, the Megarines were surely more Eloesian than they were now. *They have changed much. This must be a modern creation.*

Pointed arches surrounded the courtyard on all sides. The scent of flowers and desert plants hung thick. In some places, lizards sunbathed, having lost all fear of humans. All around, the air was thick with the scent of cooking and spice.

"Echeron!" a woman cried, startling Quartillo from his fascinated observation. A green veil covered her mouth and a blue hooded robe covered her hair. Yet judging from her nose and the tufts of curly brown hair that escaped from her clothing, she was Eloesian. The Thartans had long admired the Fharese; now, it seemed they were mimicking their customs.

What would a playwright do in such a situation? Surely he

would be pompous and proud, expecting a royal treatment. Perhaps a delegation would be expected—not just this girl. "Girl," Quartillo said with his best sneer. "Where is Gygax?"

"His Majesty is not here now," she said. "I have come to attend to your needs."

"And your name?"

"Kyra," she answered.

In the Isteroi language, it meant simply "girl." This woman was a slave, perhaps purchased in the markets of Nissos. Such a beauty would fetch several hundred *doukon*. The Thenoans had banished slavery and one year, King Gygax's father had put the matter of abolishing slavery to a vote. The citizens had rejected it soundly—at least, those citizens who could vote—and the institution of slavery remained engrained. Quartillo had much sympathy for this "Girl," this "Kyra," but would Echeron? Perhaps. "I see you are a slave," said Quartillo. "I am from Thénai you know. There are no slaves in Thénai."

Kyra looked down and stirred uncomfortably. What could such a "Kyra" do in this situation? Rebellion would not be tolerated. Tharta might have the most liberal policy toward slaves of all slave-owning societies, but her owner would not refrain from using the switch. And if she was a slave of the court, was there any law that Gygax could not break?

"I will want to look around a bit," said Quartillo. "Please leave me."

Overhead, the sky had turned cloudy, a shade of white, and the wind began picking up speed. The winter rains had arrived.

There was a big task ahead of Quartillo, and so few ways to accomplish it.

THE HOUSE OF THE ARCHON, THÉNAI

For the third time of the evening, Theron vomited into a pail. He had broken out into cold sweats and could scarcely think or breathe. The fever threatened to kill him. The infection of his wounds had begun to recede, with the careful help of his doctor, but the fever showed no signs of relenting. He had begun dreaming strange things in his sleep. He had dreamed of his life before he became archon; of his parents long dead. His mother was not herself. "You fool," she had said, "you will amount to nothing." His father called him weak and unfit. The family dog growled and barked at him. He was a stranger now—to them and to himself. *How can I possibly be archon?*

He shivered with cold, though blankets were piled on top of him. The replacement had already been chosen; it seemed that the Assembly was merely waiting for him to die. And surely he would die.

He would descend into the darkness of the underworld; he would join the mourning shades as they floated through the river. His days there would be dark and gloomy; but at least, he would not have such pain. He could not imagine the underworld being any worse than this.

Would he ever walk again? Would he even survive the night? He could not say. The world had come undone.

THE PALACE, THARTA

Out of the courtyard, within the palace's labyrinthine corridors and halls, Quartillo found himself in a world he had never dreamed of seeing. Here were items of priceless value—jewelry in glass display cases, necklaces of electrum and gold and silver, bracelets encrusted with white diamonds, blue sapphires and rubies as red as flame. Here were gold-framed paintings by the greatest artists throughout history—one especially caught his eye, a painting that took up an entire wall which dwarfed every person that walked in it. The subject was a great battle between amazon and Eloesian. Quartillo stopped there and observed it: on one side the swarthy, dark-haired amazon women with glaives and clubs, on the other Eloesian men nude save for helmets and bronze greaves, thrusting out spears and hurling javelins. In the center of the picture was the amazon queen Phoebë dying, pierced through by a javelin.

The playwright Antillēs had written of this historical battle: the Battle of Myrtle Field, when the amazons were finally driven from the Eloesian heartland and into the coastal islands. As with all plays, the action took place off-stage; the play had focused on the politics of pre-democratic Eloesus, and the impending revolt by the people against the kings.

"Amazing work, is it not?"

Quartillo leapt at the voice. It was deep, with a twinge of a foreign accent. Quartillo turned to meet it and found the vizier standing there. The vizier—Khusruh was his name—wore a tiered triangular headdress of gold and long silken robes dyed purple. His complexion was near black and clearly he was old, yet his face was fresh and youthful, even handsome. Here was the second most powerful person in the world after the King of Kings himself. Ought not Quartillo tremble? Shouldn't he be quivering and begging for mercy? Could this vizier see through his schemes?

Could he see through the role Quartillo had prepared?

"It is all right," the vizier said. "You do not need to respond. I am used to people quaking at my presence." He laughed, and there Quartillo saw gold in his teeth. So wealthy was this vizier that he could replace his teeth with gold.

"I am Echeron," Quartillo lied. He sought a place deep within himself, a place of pure imagination. To be a successful mimic, he had to inhabit the mind of another—to become, fully and totally, another human being. It would be difficult, some might say impossible. But this was the whole purpose of the Mysterium. This was his reason for being.

"Echeron," the vizier repeated. "You are a writer of plays, no?"

Quartillo nodded. *I am Echeron, the writer of "The Owls" and "The Seventh Son."* No more was he Quartillo; he had to leave that persona behind. Goodbye, Quartillo; hello, Echeron.

"I confess I am not a watcher of plays," said the vizier. "You will find that drama is not a common thing in the world. I daresay it makes Eloesus strange."

By Amara, he does not like Eloesus. I can hear his derision. Echeron forced a smile. "That is likely true. But in Eloesus drama is the great unifier. Even the poor like watching them. That is why I write…"

The vizier laughed in a way that was almost a sneer. "Ah. Well, my dear Echeron. That may be so. In Fharas, the low know their place; it is not with the high. Some are meant to toil in the fields and craft tools and artworks. Others live and rule in palaces— it is the natural order of things."

For a moment, Echeron left and Quartillo returned; the jewels and wealth that the vizier brought with him were surely somewhere. That is why he had come; were there a pair of keys to steal? He gazed at the silk robe and saw nothing save for a cloth sash tied tight around his waist. He met the vizier's gaze and saw dark eyes that did not hide their scorn. Everything about Eloesus was beneath him; even in this palace, in Tharta, amid this wealth. And yet it seemed he liked Echeron, strange as it was, the low-born son of a sandalmaker who became a great playwright. The gaze became overbearing. "It was an honor beyond what I deserve to meet you, Your Worship," said Echeron. "May you and your lord live forever."

"Athra willing, we will," said the vizier.

There was something on the tip of his tongue, something he wanted to say and knew he couldn't. Was it "we will live forever, but this small and pitiful land will not."

THE HIGH PORCH, THARTAN PALACE

Gygax's nerves twisted to knots as he waited for his bride. The wedding guests crowded the high porch, which jutted out from the palace and overlooked the gray sea. Far below, the din of the streets echoed upward: the faint sounds of carriages rattling, merchants shouting, and the barking of dogs.

Gygax had agreed to perform the wedding in accordance with Zubeida's wishes. He still had not seen his new wife's face. Her mother sat at the front of the porch, dressed in all black like her daughter, but showing her face—harsh, wizened features, olive skin and dark eyebrows. A large mole was near her mouth and her eyes were dark and unremitting. She did not drink wine or eat beef. She had not spoken a word to Gygax since her arrival. Gygax knew practically nothing about her; only that her name was Bat Zor, that she came from the land of the "Shakrathites," that the women of that land did not drink wine only water, and that of all the hundred wives of the King of Kings, she was the most revered. A smattering of servants and family members sat near her, in addition to the vizier Khusruh. On the other side were Gygax's family and servants, dressed modestly in accordance with the wishes of Bat Zor.

It was not a magus—one of the legendary fire priests of Fharas—that stood there but instead a man in animal hides and a horned cap, a priest of Nawäl, the Shakrathite god. The magi accompanying the party sat in the back, wearing purple silken robes and white turbans, laying their shepherds' crooks across their laps. They, representing the most widespread faith of Fharas—the fire god Athra—accompanied all the King of Kings' emissaries, for they had not only religious zealotry but vast magical power.

In accordance with the customs of the Shakrathites there was no music, either. It made everything seem so grim. And yet Gygax did not regret his decision, not yet. This marriage would sow him into the fabric of the Fharese Empire, into the very heart of it. He would ally the Thartan royalty with the victors; they would never fear the King of Kings' wrath.

The priest of Nawäl lifted up a plain leaden goblet. Water splashed from it. "Come, bride!" he howled in strained Eloesian. "Come, flower! Come, precious lily!"

The doors to the porch opened and Zubeida appeared, dressed completely in black. The Fharese party stood up in their seats, and the Eloesian party followed a second later. Her father was not there to escort her; he was, by all appearances, too busy. She walked gracefully and—at her sight, women from both the Eloesian and Fharese parties began tossing flowers and bundles of sweet-smelling plants. Soon the porch smelled of mint and jasmine.

"Come, bride!" the Fharese party chanted, and the Eloesians joined in. "Come, flower! Come, precious lily!"

She stepped on the dry aromatic bundles and the air grew even thicker with the sweet, refreshing scent. Gygax was more nervous than ever. He still had not seen her face, nor spoken a word with her.

"Come, bride!" they chanted. "Come, flower! Come, precious lily!"

Gygax wanted to run. He could not help but feel unmanly for all these nerves. What did she look like? What was she hiding? Had Gygax made a terrible mistake?

"Come, bride! Come, flower! Come, precious lily!"

She pivoted to face him. Through the mesh that hid her face, Gygax could make out the faint shadows of eyes and a mouth, a nose, and cheekbones.

"You are joined in matrimony!" the priest of Nawäl

shouted. "I declare Gygax and Zubeida one! Drink!"

He held the lead goblet to Gygax's lips, and he drank deep of the sickeningly metallic water. Zubeida followed. Then, to his surprise, she tore off her veil.

She revealed a face more beautiful than Gygax ever expected; a face youthful and fresh, olive skinned but darker than her mother, brown eyes the color of almonds, tender red lips and a thin nose. She was far more beautiful than Gygax's first wife Thelema. All Gygax's regrets vanished. All his second thoughts evaporated.

"And now shall the virgin bride mate!" the priest of Nawäl. "Now shall they meet in animal frenzy!"

The Fharese party began shouting. They were speaking the Shakrathite tongue, which Gygax did not know. The Eloesians joined them, a second late as always. They lifted up both Gygax and Zubeida. They carried them out of the porch, through the palace's corridors and walkways, and to the marriage bed.

THE HIGH PORCH, THARTAN PALACE

Late at night, Echeron returned to the sight of the scandal. He had not realized, all this time, that King Gygax was still married to Queen Thelema. Never before in Eloesian history had a king married more than one wife. It was a first, and ripe for drama. He would have ample fuel for his next play.

Zubeida or Thelema—whom would he favor more? Already he had five children by Thelema, and one daughter by Yvonna, whom he had divorced. Some might say he had taken Fharaizing too far, breaking every Eloesian custom in an effort to bring Tharta into the southron fold.

Echeron walked out into the cold air of the High Porch. The chairs sat empty and abandoned. He was alone. He had time to take off the mask, to become Quartillo once again. For all the scandal and shock of what had gone on, his mission had not changed; he needed to find his way into the Fharese party's quarters. He needed to take their treasure. They were leaving tomorrow. The queen, Bat Zor, would be gone. So, too, would the vizier.

A shooting star streaked across the sky, brilliant in its color. Quartillo heard the door open behind him. He gazed at the sky, pretending not to notice. He put on the mask of Echeron once more.

"You know," said the booming voice of the vizier, "the wise of my country believe the answers to everything are written in the stars, if you look hard enough."

Echeron turned to look at the vizier, who stood half again his height. "Everything, you say." He gazed into those dark eyes, seeking answers not in the heavens. There was something suspicious in the Fharese visit. Why would the vizier attend the wedding of a princess? Why would the King of Kings' chief advisor attend? What were they hiding?

"Bat Zor did not want to come," said the vizier.

Echeron could not forget the harsh-featured, harsh-mannered mother of the princess. She would not speak to anyone, not even if they approached her.

"She has nurtured a hatred of Eloesus from the beginning," he continued. "The concept of democracy has long enraged her."

Tharta was the least democratic of all Eloesian cities. Their democracy was intermittent, holding votes over this or that law. Nothing of importance was ever decided by the people.

"She was never comfortable with the marriage."

Echeron turned. The vizier laid a hand on his shoulder. Echeron bristled slightly at the touch. He did not trust this man, nor any southrons. They were violent, it was said, and domineering and cruel. They turned kingdoms to nothing and burned civilizations to ash. "What do you see in the stars?" Echeron asked.

The vizier left him, walking ahead to the edge of the porch. He breathed in the cold night air. "I see a new age dawning. I see the old things passing away. I see the Goat receding from the heavens and making way for the Horse."

The Fharese had their own ideas about astrology and different names for the constellations. Quartillo had been born under the sign of the Archer; what was Echeron born under? The Twins, he decided. "Why did Zubeida marry Gygax if her mother didn't approve?" His words surprised him.

"Her father did. He thought it was… how shall I say this? Politically expedient," the vizier said. "He has great plans."

"Surely, there were wealthier nations to marry into…"

"Maybe. But Eloesus alone has refused to call the King of Kings its god. Eloesus alone has refused to heed his decrees…"

"We don't take well to decrees," said Echeron. Still, he

puzzled at the action. If—compared to Eloesus—the King of Kings had wealth beyond compare, why would he focus on Gygax? Why Tharta? Why marry the daughter of his chief wife to a nation of goatherds and philosophers?

"You Eloesians are a strange lot in many ways," said the vizier, still gazing at the stars. "You will come around, in time."

What did that mean? "Maybe," said Echeron. "Maybe not."

"You surely will," the vizier continued.

The vizier turned around and in the light of the moon and stars, metal gleamed—the edge of a key, just barely visible through a robe pocket.

"I fear for you, Echeron, that Tharta's so-called 'Fharaizing' has just begun. Temples to Athra will be built… and shrines to Nawäl the Horned One. Your men will dress in robes… your women will learn to cover their hair. The theaters will be closed. All bad books will be burned—and the harmful bits of your history will be erased. And for once, your so-called citizens—what other nations call impoverished rabble—will have no say in it."

Echeron didn't know how to respond. "Well," he stammered, "I live in Thénai."

"Thénai will not escape it," said Khusruh. His dark eyes glinted in the light of the moon. "Bat Zor is a determined woman. She never forgets and she never forgives."

Bat Zor is not the queen of Thénai, Echeron wanted to say. *Or even Tharta.* He decided to let Khusruh's careless comment slip by. "Either way I suppose I must go. Perhaps there is little hope for me here… I am a playwright. If you close all the theaters I will have nowhere to go."

"Perhaps it is best that you learned a useful trade," Khusruh said. He smiled and his eyes were taunting. "A maker of sandals is of much more worth to the King of Kings than a maker of plays. Things of idle fancy are no concern to him. Tent-making or tanning… dyeing or sewing. You will find something in this new world, I am sure."

And what a grim world was this. Quartillo wondered what Echeron would do. Surely a proud playwright, wealthy and well-regarded across Eloesus, would be enraged at the prospect. But even he would not respond rudely to the Vizier of Fharas, the King of Kings' own puppet. Punishments in Fharas were severe—a thief lost an arm, a spy an ear, and a scoffer a tongue. Echeron wanted to keep his tongue, even at the cost of his dignity.

"I fear I must go," said Khusruh.

"You have a long journey," Echeron mumbled, glaring at Khusruh openly.

"I am staying here." Khusruh smiled, knowing full well how deeply that angered him. "Bat Zor is bidding her daughter farewell; but Tharta will benefit from my presence for the time being." He walked away. "Goodbye, playwright."

Like a viper biting at its prey, Quartillo snatched the key from Khusruh's robe and drew his hand away just as fast. He pocketed it quietly, watching the vizier disappear into the palace's dim corridors. Again he became Echeron, thinking like him, acting like him.

THE ROYAL CHAMBER, THARTAN PALACE

Exhausted from their lovemaking, Zubeida had fallen asleep naked in the royal bed. Gygax couldn't imagine why anyone so beautiful would want to cover her body. He sipped some wine at his bedside, emptying the last of the goblet into his throat. He wiped his sweat-covered forehead.

There was a knock at the door. *How could anyone be so rude?* "Leave me alone or I'll have you hanged!" he howled.

At the words, the knocker kicked open the door outright, revealing the form of Bat Zor. Gygax's anger melted into panic as he beheld her harsh crone's face. In her black gown she seemed to glide like a ghost. "I have come to bid my son-in-law goodbye," Bat Zor said. The tone of her voice itself was threatening. "I have sacrificed much. My daughter is marrying outside the empire. I will not see her for a long while."

Like a wraith she had glided across the room. Gygax hid his nakedness with a blanket.

 She touched the empty wineglass. "You have been drinking," said Bat Zor. "I can also smell it on your breath. If you ever have my daughter drink some, you will regret it. Did she taste any?"

A swallow. "No," Gygax lied.

"She has been pure of wine and men her entire life."

She has drunk before, she told me. And she did not bleed when we made love.

"I expect little from a heathen," Bat Zor said. "But the purity of a Shakrathite woman must be guarded. No wine must touch her lips. No beef can be eaten. Outside her bedchamber she must be covered head to toe."

OUTSIDE THE WATER NYMPH WING, THARTAN PALACE

Echeron had been put aside; he was purely Quartillo now. Echeron would not dare enter the Water Nymph Wing, where all the Fharese guests were gathered. He had watched carefully; the guards posted at the door had taken a brief break. It seemed there were limits to even the guards' patience.

Quiet and breathless, Echeron opened the door and entered a gloomy room.

~

The lanterns had been put out; the hallways were dark, and the paintings of dolphins and undersea nymphs were barely distinguishable. Quartillo's heart was pounding inside his chest. He wondered if the vizier might have noticed his missing keys. He wondered if the Fharese had a second sight or the ears of dogs, and would all startle awake as soon as he passed by their room.

He peered quietly into an open doorway and saw a rug spread across a wooden floor. Dozens of girls—perhaps handmaids—lay sprawled around and snoring. He quietly passed them by.

In another room were men sleeping on cots, dressed only in their underclothes, with feathered turbans clutched nearby. He scanned the room for bags of any kind; he saw great wooden chests and paused a moment. Cautiously he approached, stepping over sleeping bodies, cognizant of the fact that death could be seconds away. Heart pounding, he opened one chest—and found a dozen pipes, sitting on a pile of cloths.

He wanted to curse but dared not. He stepped across the bodies once again, holding his breath, not daring to inhale or exhale. He entered the hall once again… and bumped into a woman.

She was garbed in all black, with only her face uncovered. Her features were severe and wizened, with a mole near her lips. Her eyes were dark, and yet there was a glow to them—green in color, eldritch, like an enchantress was said to have.

Quartillo felt strangely calm. He did not understand why he wasn't running. In fact, he found himself unable to move. "Who—" he managed to whisper, but all other words had left him.

"Bat Zor," the woman said and smiled. "Come with me, child… I know what you are looking for."

Quartillo followed her down the hall. She moved smoothly, like a disembodied ghost. It seemed she did not step or move her legs as she walked.

At the far end of the hallway, she ushered him inside.

Two guards with sabers were snoring on the ground. They were not dressed for sleeping; they still wore their iron helmets and skirts of mail.

Ahead, on a large bed, the vizier was sleeping.

"Go," Bat Zor whispered. "See those boxes? There you will find what you are looking for…"

Large wooden chests with keyholes were stacked on top of one another.

"I… Why?" Quartillo couldn't believe all this was happening.

"You would have had no chance without me," Bat Zor whispered. "Those guards would have killed you on sight."

Bat Zor pushed him on. He ambled through the room, past the snoring bodies, beside the bed where the vizier lay. He fitted the key to the chest and opened it, finding it filled to the top with glittering gold and jewels.

"Such wealth is nothing compared to what the King of Kings spends daily at his household." Bat Zor was right behind him. "Go on; take as much as you'd like."

After a moment's hesitation, Quartillo began piling the gold and jewels into bags he had brought.

"Your plan was so foolish. It is good that I was here."

Quartillo could not believe his luck. When both bags were heavy with gold and jewels, he turned to leave.

"Ah," said Bat Zor, "but there is one thing you've forgotten. The most valuable thing that you will take."

She took the key from him and opened a chest stacked high with papers. They were written in Fharese.

"I can't read those," said Quartillo.

"But someone else might," answered Bat Zor.

Out of thanks for her generosity and help, Quartillo began filling the already-heavy bags with papers, until he had taken them all. Then he stood up and stared into Bat Zor's bewitching eyes. "Why?" he asked.

"There are things you are not meant to know," said Bat Zor. "There are reasons you would not understand. Remember me, Quartillo, in the trouble ahead… Remember me…"

THE FATTENED PIG, POTTERS' DISTRICT, THARTA

The journey home had taken less than a half hour, but it seemed he had traveled to a different world. The poverty here was omnipresent. The patrons of The Fattened Pig dressed in grays and browns, some in tattered rags, helping themselves to bread and wine, or more often bread and water. Despite the name of the tavern, it seemed few could afford pork. The royal court ate endless feasts, while the people starved. That, Quartillo reminded himself, was the way of the world—how it was and how it always would be.

Didyma ambled in some time after noon. Something was bothering her. "Quartillo," she whispered. "The Master wants to see you… privately."

"Truly?" Quartillo knew the cause for Didyma's sadness; the Master had never asked for anyone besides her before.

"He said he 'couldn't believe you succeeded.' He wouldn't stop ranting on."

"Where—"

"You know that old, burnt out house on Old Wall Road? There is a door… Search enough and you will find it." She handed him a key.

Quartillo said, "Thanks," and turned around, wondering if—through all this lucky turn of events—he had lost a friend.

~

The burnt-out shell of a house had stood there for as long as any could remember, and no city official had cared enough to tear it down. The Old Wall Road was lined with decaying buildings and abandoned homes. The road was of dirt, and after a rainstorm it would become muddy and unnavigable.

From here, like most parts of Tharta, he could see the High City—the temple to Alabastros gleaming white in marble on a towering rock plateau. He gave one last thought to that splendid world he had left. Gone were the rich feasts, the musical performances, the days of drama at the theater. The squalor of the Potters' District was Quartillo's home; he was no Echeron.

He stepped carefully through the rubble of the burnt-out house. It took a thief's eye to find the door, but he did find it—a trapdoor that seemed to blend in with the rubble, complete with the keyhole.

His nerves were twisting to knots. He did not want to meet the Master. He did not want to be judged by the greatest of the Mysterium. He was not worthy to be here—all his success was due to the treachery of Bat Zor. He owed none of it to himself.

He fit the key into the trapdoor and opened it. Musty air met him as he climbed down and shut the trapdoor behind him, entering a cavernous world.

~

Lamps burned throughout the rock corridors, glistening on the jagged stone. The floor was unsteady, misshapen and composed of dirt. He made his way through the musty, twisting corridors.

At last he came to a door—a voice said "Come in!" and it opened all by itself. Quartillo took those nervous steps inside, into a brightly lit room.

The Master sat at a desk. He wore a black hood which hid his face; the bare impression of a mouth could be seen, white and aged.

Nervously, Quartillo placed the bags of gold, jewels and documents on the desk.

"You have done well," said the Master. He opened the bags.

His hands seemed far too small for his body. Come to think of it, his face looked small as well, almost like a child's.

He picked up the papers. "Fharese documents," said the Master. "Strange writing, isn't it? Looks like scribbles, hmmm? How can they read it, you wonder."

He was putting words in Quartillo's mouth. So be it.

"And yet I can read it," said the Master. "The leader of the Mysterium must know how to read all languages."

The Master began to read. Quartillo busied himself by examining the room. Here, in this chamber—carved from subterranean rock—there were countless bookshelves, holding enough scrolls for a library. Behind the Master, the stylized Eye of the Mysterium loomed high, crafted of luminous crystal.

His gaze turned to the Master himself; there was something strange about him, about his body. Something just wasn't right about him.

"My word," said the Master, "you have done well. Well enough to make you the new Deputy."

"Deputy," said Quartillo. Would he truly replace Didyma? It seemed unfair. "I—I was helped—"

"This gold will feed the Potters' District for years," said the Master, "and these documents have told me something else… true doom. Doom is coming for us, Quartillo! Doom!"

A TASK FOR A HERO

The King of Tharta built a tomb
He hewed it out of mountain rock
He told no soul where it was built
The bones of brave Phillipidēs
Were laid within its gleaming stone.

— Arkelaios

THE HOUSE OF THE ARCHON, THÉNAI

The gales of winter were blowing, the rain was pouring, and lightning was flashing when—at last—the Archon of Thénai sat up from his sickbed and decided he was well enough to walk.

Theron had wasted many months bent over in pain, suffering through agony each hour of each day. Enough was enough. The wound had begun to heal; too much movement was still excruciating, but sitting by and doing nothing was far worse.

The physician, seated beside him in the midwinter gloom, quickly protested. "You must have your rest!" he cried.

"More rest will kill me—and kill us all!" He walked out of the room, ignoring the pain and the still-tender wounds of his chest. In the main hall a fire was burning. On a hook was an oiled winter cloak. He crossed the room and grabbed it, draping it across his body. Then he walked outside.

~

The air was bitingly cold and sheets of rain were falling from the cloudy sky. From the High City, the waters of the sea were visible. The waves were towering in size, crashing against the shore. On days such as this, the burning heat of an Eloesian summer was a happy memory.

He sensed someone behind him. Who was crazy enough to follow him outside into the rainstorm?

He turned, panicking for an instant. Had the King of Tharta sent an assassin again?

But a woman stood there in a glistening cloak of Hymnian wool. She was fair in complexion, with light brown eyes and tufts of golden hair which escaped from her hood. A medallion was strung around her neck—a medallion he recognized. The bronze was forged into the shape of the bent peak of the Mount of Prophecy. Zoë—no, Io—had sent this woman.

"What do you want?" said Theron.

"The King of Kings will invade Eloesus," she said. "He has raised an army, the likes of which have never been seen before…"

There was something strange about this woman. Her voice did not sound quite right.

"He has sent his daughter to turn the King of Tharta against his Eloesian brothers… The vizier… he…" The woman fell into a coughing fit.

Theron grabbed her and the illusion was shattered. A man stood there, garbed in the cloak of oiled wool. He was thin and short and his whole presence seemed to exude untrustworthiness.

"Who are you?" Theron asked.

"I am Gaia… a handmaid of the Mount of Prophecy." With the illusion gone, he could not convince the simplest of men.

"Tell me the truth or I will have you arrested," said Theron.

"I am… I am… err…"

Guards, posted at all times on the High City, were running up to them. The rain had moistened their horsehair crests of their helmets, matting them down. "What is wrong?" one cried.

"Take this man to prison to await trial…" Theron began.

"I am Quartillo of Tharta!" the man said suddenly. "I will tell you everything. I promise, I will not lie anymore. I was sent to tell you of the coming disaster…"

"Quartillo." The name was not Eloesian. Perhaps he was a bondservant, or a descendant of one. Thartans still had the barbaric practice of slavery. "You tricked my eyes."

"It must have been something simple… the shadows… a play of the light."

No, there was power in this one. There was something this "Quartillo" was not telling him. Theron would pry it out of him, one way or another.

THE HALL OF FEASTING, THARTAN PALACE

The palace slaves brought in a hog which had been roasted whole on a spit. They began carving it before the court—a court far larger than King Gygax would like. After the scandal of the theft, Bat Zor and her party had refused to leave, claiming it showed the "great mismanagement and disarray of the Thartan Palace." Gygax had begun to despise that old woman more than anyone else in the world. He hated her almost as much as her daughter, Zubeida, did. In their private time she had given vent to all her frustrations; she thought Bat Zor was using the excuse of a robbery to exert ever more control over her, and never let her go. Zubeida had told Gygax of her great lust for a glass of wine, of her desire to break out of her thick woolen garb and dress as a "free woman."

In their nightly talks, she had told Gygax of Bat Zor's hatred for the Eloesian people. In the far-off courts of the King of Kings, Bat Zor had heard of the concept of "democracy." The thought of the common people choosing their leader, Zubeida told him, had disgusted Bat Zor; if the lower classes so much as spoke a word against the King of Kings their tongues would be cut out and their bodies flayed of skin.

The slaves, having dismembered the roasted hog, had begun laying out portions of various cuts onto silver platters. They would eat well tonight. According to Shakrathite custom, no lamb or beef was served—a lamb "was for wool," Bat Zor said, and a cow "for milk." The thought of consuming such meats was horrifying to the Shakrathite—another reason, Zubeida had told him, for Bat Zor's unending hatred.

When the king's portion arrived—a large slab of pork and several cuts of the stomach—arrived at his table, Gygax took a bite and then drank a big swallow of wine, glaring at Bat Zor all the way.

A slave came by and set out Zubeida's goblet of water. She cursed under her breath. Gygax touched her hand to comfort her.

Beside him, Thelema cleared her throat. He turned to glance at his first wife, seated to his left, whom in recent days and weeks he had practically forgotten. The idea of having more than one wife had once been abhorrent to the Eloesian mind, but no more. With Zubeida, Gygax had put aside the Eloesian—the roving goatherds of the hill—and put on the southron monarch. No more would such idle games as "limited democracy" be tried. What Gygax's Fharaizing father had began, he would complete.

As he cut away at his pork, he eyed Bat Zor, examining her every move. She had a crystal goblet of water set out before her and a small portion—per her instruction—for gluttony along with wine-drinking were impermissible for Shakrathite women. Still she wore those black woolen robes and the headdress which hid everything but her severe, wizened face. He had no doubts she was a plotter and a schemer. The reasons for her stay were far more than just this robbery; of that he was certain. What did she want?

Again, Thelema cleared her throat.

"What is it?" Gygax growled.

Thelema, three months pregnant, had tears in her eyes. She was a complainer; Gygax knew full well that her slaves took very good care of her. She would have to learn to share his affections with Zubeida. If Gygax were a southron king, such behavior would not be tolerated.

"Well?"

"'Treasure the woman of your youth,'" she quoted the Eloesian poet Himnaea. "'Do not stray. Take pleasure in her eyes, her hair, her bosom…'"

"Enough," Gygax growled. If there was one thing he could not bear, it was being made to feel guilty.

"Your children love you," Thelema said. A tear dripped down her rosy cheek. How different she looked from Zubeida; her hair was not black but the color of roses, her eyes not brown but blue like the sea. He remembered when she was younger, a maiden, never married—he had taken her hand in the High Porch, like he had with Zubeida and before, Yvonna. Her father, the King of Isteros, had been in attendance; as had his band of hoplites thirty strong, with shields and swords never leaving their grip. Thank the gods, no brawl had broken out—though the Isterosians were heavy drinkers and always belligerent. No doubt King Myno would be enraged at the thought of his son-in-law taking a second wife. Was there any greater insult to his daughter, and to himself?

For a moment, he treasured the woman of his youth—her eyes, her hair, her bosom.

Then he stood up and left.

~

The corridors of the palace had once seemed a happy place. The works of art by famed sculptors and painters had once provoked his admiration. Now, the period of peace was gone; there were so many people competing for his attention. *Perhaps, there is a reason why Eloesians only took one wife.*

Now he worried about more than just conspiracies and assassinations. His wives would be the end of him.

At last he found himself in the courtyard. The recent rains had faded and the sky above was bright blue. The sun once more beat warmly against him. The courtyard with its shrubs and plants filled the air with its perfumes—sweet lilacs and myrtles, saffron crocuses and lilies-of-the-valley, white maidenflowers and dark purple queens-of-the-evening. At least here, he would have peace. Here he would not have to worry about his wife's bickerings; he would have endless peace in this little garden. It was his sanctuary.

Then the tall dark form of the vizier appeared. His robes of gold cloth touched the ground, and the sapphires and emeralds inset within sparkled in the sun's light. His tall, hulking form barely fit through the colonnaded entryway.

Just who I don't want to see.

"Your Majesty," said the vizier. "I see you have left the feasting hall. You usually eat your noon meal, do you not?"

"It is not your concern, vizier."

"Ah, but what ails the king is always my concern." The vizier clutched one of the columns, steadying himself as he walked across the stone path and took a seat beside Gygax. "Two wives are so much trouble."

"Is it that obvious?" Gygax asked.

"A vizier must be a good reader of people," he said. "He must know what goes on behind the mask. We all wear masks, you know. Even me."

"What do you want?"

"Your children... there are six, no?"

Gygax's children were rarely seen or heard—still young, they were tended to by nurses and palace slaves. Gygax still had a strong relationship with them, especially with his eldest Phara. She would turn nine next month.

"As a king in the Fharese Empire, you have certain obligations," said the vizier. "Your children have been raised as heathens... worshippers of false gods and idols."

Gygax bristled at the term "heathen." The Eloesians had long considered all other peoples besides themselves—even the Fharese—"barbarians."

"Your children must be re-educated. I have arranged to send them to the capital, to Seshán, to learn at the feet of the magi and the satraps."

"A Fharese education." Was an Eloesian education not enough for them—lessons by the best tutors in geography, mathematics, and history? Had such an education not produced a plethora of inventions and uncovered so much truth about the world? *I am still clinging to my Eloesian heritage, I must let go.*

"I do not like the word 'education,'" said the vizier. "It is so very *eastron,* is it not? It is so very Eloesian. They will learn the art of ruling from the satraps; they will learn of the true god from the magi."

"The true god?"

"Athra, the Fire Lord," the vizier said. "You have heard of him, have you not?"

"Athra, the god of fire," said Gygax. "One god among many…"

"So has been the traditional understanding," the vizier began, "and yet some people have begun to think he is the only god worth worshipping; or the only god at all. Some say he is the True Lord, locked in a struggle with the prince of cold and darkness."

Gygax had consented to the construction of shrines and temples to Athra; would they replace all others? The temple on the High City would change its allegiance; would all the others follow? "What of Nawäl?" He did not care for the god of the Shakrathites any more than his irreligious new wife did; but perhaps the name would change the vizier's mind.

"The Lord of Shakrath is revered only there… The Nawlīm once had a shrine in Taifun but the monotheists destroyed it and drove them all out."

Taifun, no doubt the name of a city. Monotheists—what were those? There was so much for Gygax to learn, so much he did not understand. The merging of the two cultures—Fharas and Eloesus—would be full of pain and difficulty; of that, he was certain. Was it possible? He had begun to doubt it.

"Your daughters will come back Fharese," said the vizier. "They will know to dress modestly and how to behave in Fharese society. Your sons will come back strong and wise, capable of ruling the satrapy of Eloesus."

Gygax bristled at the word. "Satrapy! I govern an independent kingdom. And Eloesus is hopelessly divided. They will never form a union."

"We will see," the vizier said. "Anything is possible before the Supreme King."

CITY PRISON, THÉNAI

They had shackled the intruder—the man named Quartillo. There was no cause to execute him or even charge him a fine. Yet Theron did not want to send him away from the city.

In the dingy chambers of the prison, Theron's bodyguard had stripped Quartillo to his underclothes and rummaged through all his belongings. Among cookpots, roadbread and everything expected of a traveler, they had uncovered documents written in the Fharese language. Was there a grain of truth to the man's story? Could the King of Kings of Fharas truly be intent on ceding Eloesus?

The Eloesian army might hold them off for a month, or two, but how could they possibly resist Fharas' imperial might?

"When I looked at you at first, you were someone else," said Theron. "You changed. You had looked like a woman—a maiden of the Mount of Prophecy."

"I don't know what to tell you," Quartillo answered. "It was a trick of the light…"

"A trick of the light." Theron laughed openly. He glared at Quartillo. "I am not a fool. Do you take me as one?"

"The King of Kings is coming… he will make all of Eloesus his slave."

"That remains to be seen," said Theron. He did not understand how this Quartillo had so dramatically changed his appearance; if he was a magician, he was the least like a magician of all his brethren. He was not calm and dignified like the white theurges, nor was he zealous and wild like the hierophants. Where to place him? What to do with him? Theron really had no choice. "Let him go. Unbind his shackles."

"Do not fail Eloesus," Quartillo continued as Theron's men unlocked the shackles. "Heed the warning… Heed the warning, Theron!"

"Get out of here," Theron said and Quartillo stumbled out of the grim stone chamber.

He hoped it was the last he would see of the rat.

~

The skies had cleared and the clouds had dispersed, but the air retained its winter chill. The sunlight gleamed on the red roof tiles of homes and shops. Theron had largely recovered from his wounds, but one thing he could not seem to overcome—the feeling that he was not made for his position, that he neither deserved it nor was fit for it.

Before he rescued the city of Thénai from the demon Kronos, he had been no more than a wastrel and vagabond, a former hoplite only just barely scraping by—and relying on his friend Phaido, gods rest his soul. Now he was the archon, with all the demands and the pressures that came with it. Could he manage? Could he possibly succeed at this twisted game? He was no politician. He was no man of the law.

How he wished to escape all of this, to wander Eloesus and live by the sword once again. He missed those times with Zoë and with Phaido his dearest friend. At the thought of them, his eyes welled with tears. Phaido was dead, and Zoë was forever gone—changed into someone new. In a sense, she had died a deeper death.

Much of Thénai's streets were still of dirt. Here, just outside the city jail, the rain had turned them to mud. Other, richer cities such as Tharta and Korthos found it a sign of an "impoverished people." Physicians claimed it caused disease and plague. Would Theron do something about it, he had been asked more than once.

Thénai's wealth was not endless, like Tharta's. Its navy was the best in the world and its army was formidable, but it was not as strong as Tharta. Who could compete with Tharta, the greatest and oldest city in Eloesus? It had no equal in the world.

~

Theron took a shortcut through an alleyway and reached a paved road, but by the time he had gotten there, his chiton was soiled with mud and his sandals had grown filthy.

Here, on this broad thoroughfare, the shops and houses crowded the street and stretched ever-higher into the sky. Regulations on size and height were all but abandoned; as the city grew, its upward climb was inevitable. *The barbarian lives encamped on the earth; the civilized man makes his home in the sky.* So had a character in one of Phaido's plays described the concept.

The people seemed to make way for him as he navigated the packed thoroughfare, even the Fharese and Khazidean merchants who recognized his position of power and prestige.

The road opened up into the market square. Here, the sounds of shouting merchants were deafening. In the shadow of the High City, in the shadow of the temple, he felt smaller than before.

"Theron!" someone shouted. "Theron!"

He recognized the man in a chiton ambling up to him. His name was Hyron and he was the most senior member of the Assembly. Hours ago, he had discarded all the belongings of the captive Quartillo and taken them in for examination.

"Archon… a word," he said. "The Assembly must speak with you."

How badly Theron wanted to put aside his chiton, to never speak a word to the Assembly again.

Yet grudgingly he followed this Hyron, despite all his wishes.

~

The House of Assembly in Thénai was not a grand edifice like the one in Korthos. The architects had done their best—they had flanked it with pillars in both the Thenoan, Korthian and Megarine styles. Yet in form it was square, and small in size. It had been built in a less prosperous time, before the colonies had been planted across the sea—and even now, finances did not warrant its rebuilding. They would have to make do with the small House of Assembly, with the stresses of finances—and the debts owed to Tharta, brought up at each meeting. They had barely enough revenue to pay off the interest. The matter might be important indeed—but the talk of it bored Theron to tears. Was there any greater sign that he was not fit for this job, that the position of archon was beyond him?

Hyron led him through the open doors of the Assembly House, where a dozen guards had been posted in full regalia. Within lay the building to which he had grown far too accustomed. The colonnades opened up into a spacious room surrounded at all sides by benches three rows high. The marble floor, emblazoned with the laurel wreath symbol of Thénai, was illuminated by a skylight on the roof above. Each seat was filled, save Hyron—two hundred men, old and young, elected by popular vote. They bickered and insulted each other, cursed and fought. They rarely agreed on anything.

Yet it was somehow Theron's job to corral them, to force matters to a vote, to get things done—things which often seemed pointless. Who cared about the prices of bread and oil? Who cared about where every last *thalos* of tax money should be spent? Shouldn't a crowd two-hundred strong be able to decide something for themselves?

I am so unfit for this.

Yet when he walked into the center of the room, the two hundred were not bickering. They were quiet, some whispering amongst themselves and some totally silent.

They are afraid.

THE HOUSE OF ASSEMBLY, THÉNAI

Now he needed to find out just what they were afraid of.

He turned to face Hyron.

"Archon, our best examiners have determined the letters are authentic," he said. "The Fharese language is all sound and makes mention of things no forger would know… if you read all the papers, it is clear the King of Kings intends to invade Eloesus… to bring us, forcefully, into his sphere of influence."

Theron scanned the room. He saw faces ashen in color and afraid, on the verge of panic. These were not the faces of warriors or soldiers, but instead people without courage. The only question was how fast they would fall on their faces and worship the King of Kings. "We cannot submit to him," Theron said. "We will lose our democracy, our freedom, our liberty…"

"The King of Kings intends to raise an army… an army of a size that has never been seen before," Hyron said. "Before it, all nations will be crushed—so says the writings. We must be prepared. We must vote. Surely, we cannot stand against them. I move that we offer terms of surrender, that we accept the King of Kings' rule and live under his power."

"Traitor!" howled Nikator, a long-time veteran demiarch of the Assembly. The seventy-year-old man's face had gone a shade of cherry pink, and his raging eyes indicated absolute fury.

"There are no traitors here," howled a demiarch named Mikonos. "Only reasonable men! The King of Kings has most of the world under his sway. How can we possibly stand against him?"

Shouting erupted at all sides, some for, some against. Whether the Assembly wanted to fight or surrender could not be clear, only that tempers ran high, that nothing would be resolved, that nothing would get done. Two hundred squabbling fools—how had Theron's ancestors decided this was how to govern? How had Theron's ancestors decided this was how to run a city and a civilization, a people prosperous and numerous—albeit less prosperous and numerous than they had been?

Yet somehow it is my job to corral them, to push them for a vote. Never had Theron resented his duties more than now. Never had the position been such a grief to him, such a source of rage. How could he possibly unite these factions? How could such a large group of squabbling, petty men decide on anything?

"Enough!" shouted Theron, and his voice was so loud that the Assembly immediately hushed. For a moment, they feared their furious archon more than the threat of the King of Kings. Their faces turned ashen again; all this fury was because of desperation and fear, of near certain doom. "We will vote and for once, we will not argue!"

Even Nikator had stopped shouting; his bright red face had gone pale, revealing the utter fear behind his angry persona.

Even Theron was not immune to that fear. How could he possibly not be afraid? The greatest power in Varda, which—by many scholars' reckoning—commanded most of the world's people, wanted to force Eloesus into slavery. Resisting seemed suicide. Yet surrender was a great disgrace. What was better— bondage or disgrace? "We will vote… who says we resist, that we maintain our liberty? Who votes that we resist the King of Kings? The risks are great, but is it not better than surrender?"

Theron watched and waited. Not a single hand was raised—not even Nikator. It seemed even those who had argued against surrender were frightened sheep, willing to fight with words but never with their lives. Ashamed and disgusted of the Assembly, Theron tore off his chiton, revealing the civilian clothes beneath. "A curse on you! A curse on all of you! You cowards should be ashamed of yourselves! I forfeit my position! No longer am I an archon… I will not be a prince of frightened sheep. The proud nation of Eloesus is gone… we have become a den of cowards…"

He turned and ran out of the House of Assembly. He was leaving tonight. The Assembly wished to live in disgrace, falling prostrate before the King of Kings, but Theron would not so much as kneel. His people might be cowards, unwilling to go to war, unwilling to fight and die, but Theron would die on his feet. He would never stoop to the ground. He would curse the Fharese King of Kings to the day he died. He was born an Eloesian and he would die an Eloesian.

Tonight, he would leave the city for good.

THE INNER COURTYARD, THARTAN PALACE

The cold spell had gone and the courtyard suited Gygax well. Here, among the saffron crocuses and the fragrant flowers and bushes, he had a small sanctuary from an increasingly disturbed palace environment.

Besides the rampant jealousy between Zubeida and Thelema, the presence of Bat Zor presented all sorts of problems. She would let neither Zubeida nor Gygax out of her constant control. If Zubeida so much as touched a glass of wine, Bat Zor would unleash all her terrifying fury. Every hour of the day, she would check on Zubeida, to make sure she wore her modest black shawl—her *thawab*, which covered every part of her besides her face. The only thing that infuriated Bat Zor more than a lack of modesty was if Zubeida did not show up for her sunset worship— if she did not offer money or some small gift to the priest of Nawäl and thereby honor the god of goats. Her control seemed to grow more and more severe each day.

At night, when Zubeida and Gygax were alone, she would confide in him. She had grown so exasperated that she had talked of harming her mother—that, perhaps, the only way to stop her control was to get rid of her completely.

Personally, Gygax wondered what Bat Zor's motivations were, why she refused to relinquish control. Did she have some dark plan ahead? When he looked into those black eyes, he saw a person he did not trust, a schemer to the core. Everything she did had a motive. Everything was some facet of her control.

One thing was for certain—he had to get her out of the palace somehow, and never let her return.

He had nodded off, and only one man dared wake him, the one person who viewed himself above Gygax, besides Bat Zor—the vizier.

He stood there, wearing a thick purple robe despite the late afternoon heat.

For a moment, Gygax was angry, despite the fact that the second-most-powerful man in the world stood before him. He treasured his naps. Who was this man to stop him, even if he was the vizier of Fharas?

The towering man with skin as black as midnight wore a grim expression on his face. "Your Majesty, I am sorry…"

Only then did he notice the sounds of wailing in the background—Thelema and her handmaids.

"Your children have perished at sea."

"What?" howled Gygax. "That's impossible."

"They were loaded up in the dhow, as safe as I could make them," the vizier said. "I am sorry. The storm was too strong. The captain just barely made it to shore."

"What?" Grief seized him, mixed with anger at the thought of the captain thinking only of himself, swimming through the waves and leaving his poor children to drown. Had his life truly come to this? Instantly, he began to weep. He had not been the best father but he had loved his children deeply, though Didymos was insolent and Samos was incurably dim-witted. "This is your fault," he began to say through his sobs, "this is all your fault."

"Now don't be paranoid," said the vizier. "I will not hear accusations! Not even the best-made dhow can withstand a strong storm."

Gygax had not been accusing him of anything. It did not matter. None of it mattered. His children were gone from him, forever; was there any worse fate? Why had the gods put them on the earth, if they were meant to perish and die? He was ruined.

"But I do have good news," the vizier said. "Your wife Zubeida is with child."

Gygax wiped the many tears from his face. He rubbed his eyes. There was no joy in Zubeida's pregnancy. He had lost five precious lives today—how could he possibly be happy about a new one? Surely the baby would be stillborn, or catch ill in his first week. That was what the gods intended after all—to crush Gygax and fill his days with sorrow. *And yet I am such an easy target. Why must they sit in heaven and curse me?*

~

He could not eat or drink wine. He told Zubeida to stay away. He slept by himself, alone in his bed, as a nagging suspicion consumed him, as a thought that dared not speak its name wriggled through his mind.

THE LION'S GATE, THÉNAI

Now well-off from his position as archon, Theron left—well-equipped and well-provisioned—the town he had loved. He had put aside his chiton and all the trappings of his position. He had donned a helmet and a breastplate of bronze, and worn Pyrax in its sheath. No longer was he a cowardly politician, but a warrior. War had long been his profession. How could he stand there among the Assembly and pretend to be anything other than a man of war?

He could not hear the cowardice, the petulant bickering, the arguing and fighting, for long. He could not bear to call himself a Thenoan when the city had—by unanimous vote—decided not to defend itself and its people. How could he be one of them? How could he sully himself by staying there, among them?

He had one goal, to find the one friend who remained, the one who he had respected and had not yet died. Zoë the Amazon had become the Oracle on the Mount of Prophecy; but perhaps, if she once again saw Theron's face, she would return to him. They would wander the land once more, drawing weapons together—he, Pyrax, and she, her glaive—and it would be as it had been. No more politicking, no more talk of debt repayment and harbor maintenance, coin minting and loan interest. Theron's language had been the sword before, and so it would be again.

The High Road would take him to Arkadion and the bent, majestic peak of the Mount of Prophecy. There, he would pull his friend out from her false identity. Again he would call her Zoë, and he would call her his friend.

~

Mounted on a warhorse he had purchased through his newfound wealth, he began the journey along the High Road under circumstances he could not have dreamed of years ago.

He could not help but notice there were less travelers along the road. There were fewer merchant caravans and—throughout the hour's journey—he did not spot a single foreigner, no swarthy Fharese with black beards or copper-skinned Khazidees. A band of Isteroi from the north he saw, sporting red beards, but there was not a single southron on the road.

Could it be that the King of Kings had warned them of the ensuing blood bath? Did the Fharese emperor, whose name was equaled only by the gods, not know that he was attacking a nation of sheep? Did he not know that they would merely roll over and offer him a token of surrender and submission? He did not have to worry about a fight. The merchants should come freely to Eloesus and exploit its wealth before their master in Fharas did the same.

This was truly the beginning of the end for old Eloesus. The nation he had known was gone, vanished into the wind. A nation of warriors had been swept away, and a nation of weaklings and cowards had taken its place. Where had it gone? Or had all those friends and family members always been villains, pleased to fight Kersepoli but fleeing in panic at the sight of true danger?

A cold wind began to blow, not a sudden gust like one would expect from the nearby mountains, but slow and steady, like the exhale of a spirit. He knew this wind, blowing in from the east. Surely the wind had come from the frozen peak of the Mount of Prophecy. Its message was clear: *turn back and do your duties. You were meant to be archon.*

But how could he bring himself that low again? Could a lion ever govern a flock of sheep? Thenoans had no courage, he had come to realize. Their spirits were brittle. Their bravery was absent. They would never and could never fight Fharas. They cared only for safety; it appeared slavery was better.

The cold wind was growing stronger, pushing against him like an icy dagger. At last he stopped his horse. The wind relented. A voice cried out from behind him: "Theron."

A handmaid stood there, a young woman with tufts of brown hair straying from her hooded gown. Her face was innocent, doe-like. She held something in her hands, covered in cloth. No, it *was* cloth—it was his chiton, sewn back together by the hand of an expert seamstress. "Your Zoë is gone," she said. "She has ascended to the skies and Io has taken her place. You were given one command—to bring Eloesus together, to fight the foul King of Kings and bring him low. You must do as you are commanded. Either way, you must have this."

Was that all? Theron couldn't believe it. "No more advice? No more counsel? You will send me off with nothing more than my chiton?"

"The Oracle herself is an expert at reading destiny; yet she cannot see everything," the handmaid began. "This task is yours alone. You must rouse Eloesus, Phillipidēs. You must give your people the hearts of lions…"

She handed Theron his bundled up chiton, then turned to leave. What could Theron possibly do? He could not replace his people with courageous warriors. He could not convince the squabbling Assembly of anything, let alone of fighting a losing battle.

Yet there was a race of people who did fight, whose hearts were courageous and whose hoplites did not know fear. They were despised all across Eloesus as killers and thieves of land, as destroyers of towns, as slavers and as brutal invaders.

Could his hope lie in Kersepoli somehow?

No, it was impossible.

THE HOUSE OF ASSEMBLY, THÉNAI

After returning to Thénai in defeat, he immediately convened the Assembly. The next morning they were waiting for him—two hundred citizens, landowners able to write and read, who were elected by popular vote. They called it "democracy" but this was not the democracy that Ansolon intended, where each matter was taken up by the people and put to a popular vote. No, this was a monstrosity. *Representation, they call it—because the people cannot make good decisions by themselves.*

"I come again to you, my friends, my brothers, my fellow Eloesians…" His oratory was strained; the delivery of his rehearsed lines sounded much worse than the rendition in the mirror. "The King of Kings of Fharas is not invincible. We can drive him out. Thénai is strong… the people will fight to the death at the thought of slavery." His resolved crumbled at the sight of unconvinced faces, of disinterested frowns and scornful glares. "Our soldiers have kept away Kersepoli for decades… there is nothing to say we can't fight Fharas. I beg you, let us resist him… let us put it to a vote."

Hyron stood up. "You have returned despite all your petty words," he said. "You have returned without a hint of shame. I had hoped for something reasonable, some proposition you might have that we could possibly take up. To resist Fharas is unspeakably foolish. I cannot believe that you would even think of suggesting it!"

Theron wore his scorn openly. "You may be a coward, but I am not. If Eloesus unites… if it joins forces…"

Several demiarchs laughed. One named Staimo leapt to his feet. "We will stand shoulder to shoulder with arrogant Thartans?

With Korthians, a band of tinkerers and drunkards? With Kersepolans, infant killers, who rape women and sell young babes into slavery? With Isteroi—red-beards without any culture or sophistication? You have gone mad, Theron! You have lost your mind! That much is clear!"

"Yes, truly, we must," Theron answered, somehow managing to speak calmly. "We must unite with all the cities we have grown to hate. We must unite with tinkerers and arrogant Thartans and slavers, because the alternative is far worse. A nation without free thought, without the sciences... a nation led by a tyrant king whose word is law."

"Better a turban than a Thartan crown," said Staimo. "Better a Fharese king than a Kersepolan killer or a Korthian fool!"

"The city I had loved is gone," said Theron. As archon he had little power without the consent of the Assembly. He could not override them.

He turned and walked out of the Assembly for a second time, burdened by his failure.

~

When he viewed the streets of Thénai, he could see children playing. What future was there for them? Were they destined to live in slavery? How much would they fetch? A *doukon* a head? The Assembly thought a surrender would appease the King of Kings, but could the Fharese ever truly be trusted?

He had to seek support elsewhere. He would have to visit a place which every Eloesian feared, which every Eloesian did their best to avoid: Kersica, the land of slavery and perpetual war. It stole land from weak cities and had erased civilizations from history. They were bloodthirsty, they were vicious, they were—perhaps— irredeemable, but under no circumstances would their Assembly vote to surrender. They would rather die than submit to the King of Kings. They were slavers, but they were never slaves.

THE BORDER OF THENOA AND KERSICA

A bridge spanned a river that could scarcely bear the name.

Here, in the hot, flat plains of Kersica, the brown stream flanked by sedges wound its way through the rain-starved earth. In many ways, Eloesus was not a blessed land; few places were fit for growing food. Tharta alone had rich soils, which were responsible for its untold wealth. Many ideologues from Thénai said that Kersica—having just as poor farmland as itself—was only so wealthy by the spoils of war. One by one the cities had fallen to Kersepoli, one by one the treasuries had been raided, one by one the people had been taken slave; but soon they would have no more cities weak enough to conquer. Their luck would run out; the sources of their wealth and their spoil would vanish. They would crumble.

So they had said over and over again, for many years going back to long before Theron was born. They had been wrong then and they would be wrong now. Kersepoli remained strong, the most powerful army in Eloesus. Korthos and Thénai had held out against their might; but how much longer?

With no small amount of nervousness, Theron clucked and urged his horse on. Even the horse seemed to hesitate a bit before trotting ahead, across the ill-built and neglected wooden bridge. The dirty stream which formed the border of Thenoa and Kersica fell away behind him. He rode ahead in the warmth of the sun, finding himself in a land that all men feared.

~

Few traveled these roads. Even in peace, the Fharese

merchants with their beards and turbans did not dare to sell their silks, their incense and myrrh, their spices and porcelain cups. Perhaps even foreigners feared the slavers. The Kersepolans put even the Eloesians to the rod and whip—Eloesians, who by nature deserved freedom. How could they then refuse to collar Fharese, to brand them with the "S" of slavery?

Three days had passed across the lonely roads before the first sign of civilization emerged—pastures and flocks of sheep, towns on hilltops, clusters of palm trees around stagnant ponds. There was even a vineyard, where slaves were working.

Dozens of them, in fact, were stomping in winepresses. These Eloesian slaves, forming a vast underclass, were called Elehoi. They all wore collars as symbols of their submission. Their faces whitened as one of their Kersepolan masters walked by patting a whip.

In Thénai, it was claimed that on one day of each year, the Kersepolans would declare war on the Elehoi, beat them savagely and kill a handful in each village. A perpetual state of fear drove them to work and some, to suicide.

He stopped and paused, perhaps longer than he should. The slaver whipping them was an Eloesian as the ones he abused. A large belly hung over his woolen pants; evidently he ate and drank what these slaves grew.

"Hail! Stranger!"

Panic seized Theron. His first urge was to gallop away, but he stopped himself. He turned and viewed the threat—a man in a bronze breastplate, with an iron helmet and a red horsehair crest. A hoplite, no doubt. But was not every Kersepolan citizen a hoplite?

"What brings you to Carchedon?"

"I am on official business," Theron explained, frantic. "I

am the Archon of Thénai."

"You do not know your way around here, I see." The hoplite's face was wet with sweat from the hot sun. "Carchedon is far from the city."

Theron had not dared to ask for directions.

"Careful, or you might end up an Elehoi."

How badly Theron wanted to lecture him on their barbaric practice, to tell of what a horrible injustice they had wrought. Eloesians were by nature, free; to enslave them was against the order of things. Slavery had long been banned in Thénai, but those who practiced it should surely only limit it to barbarians.

The hoplite laughed. "No, we do not make Elehoi of Thenoans… much less the archon."

Theron wanted to cut the smile off his face with Pyrax. Surely, Carchedon was once a free town, perhaps even a large one; yet the people had been reduced to slavery and the walls tossed away stone by stone. All the dreams of its citizens had vanished; all the philosophers, the explorers, the farmers, the inventors—they and all their descendants had been bound in a collar, a shameful "S" branded on their skin with a hot iron.

"You must take the road south—it will branch into correct one if you take it long enough," the hoplite said. "The kings will not make it easy to hear an audience… especially not one without a proper retinue."

Indeed, what public official would travel alone? *Only one who had been abandoned by his Assembly and men of rank.*

"Tell them Timos from Carchedon sent you. They will know my name."

The kings—yes, Kersepoli at all times had two kings, elected by the military. They had not spoken to an Archon of Thénai from ages. All diplomacy had been banned; Kersepoli's ambassadors had been censured, expelled wherever they might be found and threatened with arrest. Kersepoli and Tharta had never been friends, but they had become the worst of enemies.

The Assembly would erupt in rage at Theron's quest, if they knew the slightest bit about it.

"Thank you, Timos," Theron said, and went on his way.

~

Through this bleak land Theron traveled, beside tiny villages and forgotten outposts on these flat, treeless plain. It was many days before the city of Kersepoli appeared. No archon or official of Thénai had seen it in many years.

Its walls seemed to stretch to the heavens. Each immense stone slab was perfectly fitted. It looked a hundred feet tall, impregnable and impossible to breach. Along the top of the walls, creatures out of nightmares had been carved: men with the tentacles of octopi; Saurians; and demons of hell. If anyone doubted Kersepoli's evil, he needed only to look at what their stonemasons had carved.

A nervousness was welling up inside Theron. A feeling of doom hovered above him. He had faced the amazons, but who could stand before these people—men who ate, drank and breathed war, who enslaved free Eloesians, whose women were as bloodthirsty and warlike as their men.

A high rock plateau stretched twice the height of the walls. There, among the heavens, was a pillared temple of white marble. The Kersepolans worshiped the god Tyros, lord of war—how fitting.

~

The gatekeeper was a giant of a man, standing six feet tall

and wearing an oversized breastplate of bronze fitted just for him. In one hand he held a giant flail; with the other he patted the handle. No one else was at the gate, trying to enter the city; only Theron was foolish enough.

"State your business," he growled. The Kersepolan accent was curt, abrasive—very fitting.

"I am from Thénai," said Theron, "on official business. I must see your k—"

The gatekeeper lifted up a hand, covered in a spiked gauntlet. There was shouting high above, and the sound of spinning wheels. The gates opened, just enough to let Theron and his horse by. Theron took a step forward, a step into the unknown, into the abyss.

Theron had expected grim barracks like those he had seen in the open plain—clusters of tents with young boys practicing swords and shields, sprinting and maneuvers. Instead he found a city not totally unlike Thénai. Amid the paved streets, women walked with young toddling children, carrying baskets of vegetables and meat or buckets of water. Some chatted with each other on the quiet street corners. Noticeably absent were men and older boys.

Theron thought he knew why; all boys who survived infancy were sent to train as hoplites. The men were posted at fortresses and towns far from the city; here, women ruled the roost.

They seemed to take no notice of him as he trotted down the impeccably clean streets. Women here had more freedom than other city-states; in some conservative societies such as Tharta it was a scandal that women were permitted to walk about the streets alone, without their father or husband. Even in Thénai, it was something slightly shocking.

In a city square, in the shadow of the High City and the

temple of Tyros, vendors had set up stalls. A fishmonger was selling the catches of the day—nets filled with still-squirming fish. Others sold greens or dried fruits. The women openly associated with these merchants, remarking on the weather or inquiring about the freshness of the goods. The young children accompanied them—boys wearing nothing more than a loin cloth, girls covered head to toe in a stifling dress. Only the adult women looked comfortable; some wore clothing that would be scandalous in Thénai, tight-fitting skirts that rose far above the knee and top pieces that revealed much of the breasts.

A great commotion was underway as Theron passed through; a woman screaming hysterically. "No!" she cried. "No, you will not take my Nikon!"

Two adult hoplites in bronze breastplates and horsehair-crested helms were trying to drag away a boy. His mother was the one screaming, holding onto one of his arms and struggling with all her might. "All men must serve!" shouted a hoplite.

"He is not a man!" cried the woman. "He is a boy, my boy. You will not take my Nikon!"

"All men must serve!" the hoplite repeated, louder and without any trace of patience. "He is no longer your son! He is a child of the State. He is a hoplite now, a Kersepolan."

"He is my son!" the woman howled. "I will not let you take him! He is my child! He will not be a hoplite! He will not die!"

The hoplites at last managed to break free of her desperate grip. She fell to her knees and began to bawl. Her black hair was disheveled; her makeup and cosmetic powders were smeared with tears.

As the hoplites led the frightened boy away, Theron wondered if this was a common scene, if mothers in Kersepoli retained their innate instincts—if they all wanted to keep their children, to see them live and prosper, and not be taken away and turned into hoplites as wards of the state. Was this the last time the woman would see her blessed son Nikon? Theron had a feeling it was.

At the base of the High City where the temple to Tyros was built, Theron found the law courts and—set against the rock wall—the pillared residence of Kersepoli's two kings. Would he find them there? Would they stoop so low as to hear the Archon of Thénai's voice? Would they trust the word of a Thenoan, and believe that the Fharese were coming?

He wondered if the word of a Thenoan was worth half the value of a Kersepolan. In some ancient laws—which Thénai had abandoned—the testimony of an outsider was worth half of a citizen's, and the testimony of a barbarian one-tenth. Surely, Kersepoli—which viewed free Eloesians as worthy of enslavement—would consider Theron's testimony worth nothing. *The Fharese are coming, oh yes, certainly*—he could hear their disdainful voices now. Then, perhaps, they would bind his hands and sell him in the slave markets of Nissos. They would brand him with a letter "S" and he—the Archon of Thénai—would spend his short life as a laborer in some foreign land.

A colonnade led to the palace's double doors, interspersed with flowering bushes and dwarf palms. With white-plastered walls and statues of nymphs flanking the doorway, it seemed that the kings of Kersepoli—having heard their reputation as violent brigands—were trying hard to impress.

Guards stood at the gate, ten in all. Tall horsehair crests stretched from their helms in bright greens and reds. Their bronze breastplates were forged in the shape of muscular chests. Heavy shields were in their left hands; spears in their right. These were Kersepolans, the most fearless soldiers in Eloesus. Theron could never intimidate them nor fight past them. He would have to beg.

"Who are you?" grunted one, the captain of the party

judging by his gold-enameled breastplate.

"I am—"

"Stop," the captain ordered. "We do not speak to a man on a horse. The kings' guard will not be looked down upon by anyone."

Theron obeyed in an instant, hopping off the saddle. His sword, Pyrax, was still visible, dangling from his belt in a leather sheath.

"Remove your weapon," the captain ordered.

Frightened by the captain's glaring eyes, Theron obeyed, unfastening his belt entirely and allowing it to hit the floor. "I am the Archon of Thénai," he said. "I must speak with your kings—or, at least, one of them."

"Our relations with Thénai are frozen," the captain said. "That is as you wish. No archon has been sent here in decades. I think you are a liar… and you know what we do with liars in Kersepoli? We cut out their tongues…"

"I promise. Do you see this chiton? It is authentic… it means I am archon. It means I am telling the truth."

The captain's glare had not lessened at all. His lips still tucked into a snarl, he said, "Perhaps. I doubt anyone would lie to the kings' guard. Nonetheless, I do not trust you."

"Timos sent me."

"Who is Timos?" the captain said.

Theron's hope began to fade. He wondered if he would never speak with the kings, if all his plans would come to nothing. Had he really traveled hundreds of miles to no avail? It seemed so unfair…

"You will enter the kings' presence," the captain said. "You will enter as all foreign dignitaries do…" The scowl vanished, replaced with a grin.

Stripped down to his loins, hands tied behind his back and legs fastened together with rope, Theron was carried—gagged with a cloth—through the palace's grim corridors. Scarcely able to breathe, Theron tried not to think of his humiliation. *I am here for a purpose,* he told himself. *I am here for Eloesus.*

The dingy corridors opened up into a grand throne room. Two thrones carved of stone sat there, without any cloth or cushion and very little in the way of carving.

The hoplites who had carried him took turns spitting on him, then carelessly jerked the cloth free from his mouth. Panting, Theron cursed. "This is how you treat the Archon of Thénai!"

"Yes!" cried a voice. A man was walking up to Theron, wearing a scarlet cape and a loin cloth, but nothing else. On his head was a laurel wreath crown forged of gold. "Any who speak to King Sardio or King Kyrion face the same fate. The Archon of Korthos… the ambassador from Tharta. If the King of Kings came here from Fharas, he too would be bound and gagged and spat upon."

King Sardio had a sword in his hand. He was young, no older than thirty, Theron would guess.

"Where is your counterpart?"

Sardio kicked him hard. Theron cried out. "You will call me Your Majesty."

Tears of pain had welled in Theron's eyes. "Where is King Kyrion, Your Majesty?"

"He is fighting a battle," Sardio said. "Soon we will take the city of Bactris from Korthos, together with its salt mine."

Theron shook the moisture from his eyes.

"Korthos will do nothing about it," Sardio said. "They will not so much as halt trade. If they do anything, they know more lives will be lost, more cities overrun, more people taken slave." He laughed. "Korthos knows well the art of peace. They are builders of trinkets and machines, but trinkets and machines do not win wars. Thénai knows the art of peace, too, and they do not even build trinkets."

"Free me," Theron growled. "Free me now!"

Sardio laughed again. "There is no reason to."

"I came with information… information that threatens us all. There is a grave threat."

Sardio kicked again but Theron dodged out of the way, rolling a few feet across the floor. The floor itself was uneven and chipped, with worn-away tiles revealing the flagstone beneath. "Why should I believe you?"

"Don't play games," Theron said. "What I have to say is too important for that."

"Then say it."

"Free me."

Sardio cursed. "You won't be freed."

"Then you won't hear it. Take me away. I'm not changing my mind."

Sardio cursed again. He walked over and with two slashes of his sword, cut the ropes which bound Theron. He stood to his feet, balancing precariously on a loose tile. "Fharas is coming."

"Fharas," said Sardio. "Why do you think that?"

"A… spy of ours… he intercepted documents. They have laid the groundwork for an invasion," Theron said. "They intend to bring Eloesus into the imperial fold… by force."

The color had drained from Sardio's face. "Truly?"

"I want your help," said Theron. "The House of Assembly in Thénai is undecided. I want your pledge… I want your promise to fight in the war against Fharas. United, we can defeat Fharas… each city shouldering the burden: Thénai with its navy, you with your army, Korthos with its army, Tharta with its army…"

Sardio laughed, but this laugh was weak and soft. The news had clearly unsettled him. "Even if we all combined and shouldered the burden…"

We would not prevail. That is what he wanted to say. But Kersepolan martial virtues prohibited him from saying it. Would Sardio die in battle? Surely. But would he do so for such an impossible quest, such an improbable dream? It seemed not.

Sardio turned his scarlet-caped back and walked to the shadows of the throne room. He returned holding a bronze-colored ball. "What do you know of the Old Dominion?" He threw the metal ball.

Theron caught it, expecting to be crushed, but found it was as light as paper. "What do I know of the Old Dominion?" he repeated. "Not much more than any common Eloesian… a great empire which spanned the world, which fell in one hour—in fire and smoke and ash—then drowned in a sea." Theron took note of the markings, written in some foreign language he did not recognize.

"A battalion of mine was out near the border, extracting taxes from the village of Klytemna… they raided the home of a man who could not afford to pay. They brought back this ball, which weighs as light as a feather. Yet it is not just a ball."

Theron realized he was touching an artifact of a prior age, an age of wonders. This was made in the time of the Old Dominion. Every few years, someone would make a discovery. Eloesian craftsmen would puzzle over them, try to replicate them, but always fail. Eloesus and the wider world would always live in the shadow of the Old Dominion; the heights of their power would never be reached again.

"Do you see the button?"

Theron scanned the ball. He noticed a small circular protrusion at the top, barely perceptible to the naked eye. He pressed it, and the ball began to whir and shriek.

Theron dropped the ball but it remained in the air, beginning to spin rapidly. The thin metal film peeled away, revealing the raw energy beneath—a raging bolt of fiery lightning, blue in color, spitting sparks and radiating its heat throughout the room. "Gods!" Theron cursed. He wondered if it would explode. It did not look stable.

"Do not worry," said Sardio. "I showed you this for a purpose. I wanted you to know just *why* we Eloesians can never stand united… why we will always be divided and in competition."

Theron found himself inching away from the spitting, sparking orb.

"All this lightning might be put to good use," said Sardio. "The Korthians have invented a great machine, a colossus…"

Theron remembered seeing one in Korthos—a great hulking giant of metal, forged into the shape of a god, with giant fists that could bring down city walls.

"It will only work when lightning strikes," said Sardio. "Was there ever a more impractical siege weapon? Not even their hierophants can conjure a bolt strong enough. And yet, if we gave them this wonder, the colossus would work on command; none could stand against the mighty Korthians."

Sardio walked up to the blazing lightning orb. Again he pressed the button and the orb retracted. The lightning vanished as its metal surface closed in again. It struck the floor, no longer suspended in the air, and a hollow clank echoed through the room.

"Do you see why your alliance will never come to be?"

"Yes," Theron said. For the past few days it had dawned on him that cooperation was impossible, that Eloesians could never unite. They were far too busy killing and competing with each other. There would be no united front. Weak and divided, the Fharese Empire would swallow them up, one city after another. In accordance with Fharese custom, the men would be killed; the women, sold into slavery or kept in some lord's harem.

Eloesus would be a memory. The goddess Amara would be

forgotten. Theron would die—but he would die on his feet. Sardio and the demiarchs from Thénai would die on their knees.

"Kersepoli has two kings," Theron said. "One has said no. The other remains…"

Sardio laughed darkly. "You will have no better luck. Kyrion is as much a realist as I. *Take him away!*"

Theron's feet and arms were tied again. The guards spat on him and then ferried him away through the winding corridors. Now that even the courage of the Kersepolans was in doubt, it was clear Eloesus would become some scribbled note in a history book—if all memory was not erased forever.

THE PALACE, THARTA

Over the days and weeks that followed the tragedy, it had become clear that Gygax's first wife Thelema blamed him. But how could the deaths of his children, claimed by the sea, be anyone's fault but the gods?

He had taken his seat in the feasting hall for the noon meal. Great loaves of bread, three feet long, had been laid across the table, together with bowls of figs, dates, and pomegranates; jugs of wine and various cuts of pork; crispy strips of lamb, and, as always, a goblet of cold water for Gygax's second wife Zubeida. She had taken to sitting at his right side, with Thelema at his left. She had grown more lovely to him, while Thelema had grown distant and cold. The vizier made wild claims about an affair with a strange man but Gygax did not believe it. Thelema was many things—a quarrelsome and nagging wife, a spoiled Isterosian princess, an overbearing but very good mother—but she was not an adulteress. Of that, Gygax was certain.

The southrons had a custom of naming a "chief wife" by which the order of succession was established. Just weeks ago, he would have chosen Zubeida. Now, he wasn't sure. He had not lain with Thelema since their children's deaths; would she consent to another child, with the man who had betrayed her?

Having two wives was not the delight he had expected. He did not recognize the man he saw in the mirror; he saw a man with graying hair and sagging eyes, an expression on his face that was worried even in its best moments.

He drank wine, a deep gulp that emptied half the chalice. Like clockwork, Bat Zor—sitting across the room—met his gaze to offer her judgment and condescension. *Wine makes the mind feeble and the heart weak*, she was saying. *That poison will rot your bones.*

In response, he drank the rest of it, so suddenly that wine

trickled down his chin and dripped onto his royal robe. He reached for the bottle to pour himself another glass; Zubeida struck his hand and forced it to the table. "No," she whispered. "My mother… I will not hear the end of it."

Whom should he despise more? The wife who had turned against him and now hated him, or the one who tried at every moment to control him out of fear for her mother? He jerked away her hand. He poured himself a glass of wine until it reached the top of the cup. He gulped it down and fled the feasting hall. He would not be controlled. He would not be a slave to anyone. He caught Bat Zor's glaring gaze and stopped himself from spitting on her face. She had no right to manipulate the King of Tharta like a puppet—even if she was the wife of the most powerful man on earth.

~

The garden, as always, soothed Gygax's soul. Here, in the gentle heat of the sun, the scents of the various plants and bushes filled the air with spice. It was his personal paradise, his quiet sanctuary. Bat Zor could take away his self-control; she could take away his happiness and his peace; but she could not take away his garden courtyard or the healing plants that grew within. She could not take away the rows of saffron crocus or the fragrant queens-of-the-evening, his Paladian venom pitchers or his goldhair maidens. She could not take away the peace that came from the gentle warmth of the sun, the tranquility of silence, the calm and serenity of nature. Here, in his private Arkadian woods, no one could bother him.

A voice woke him from his delusion: "Your Majesty."

Gygax cursed. He did not care if it was a god at the edge of the garden; he did not want to be bothered.

"I have news."

Gygax cursed again. "Can't you see you aren't welcome?"

He turned and found one of the less significant members of the court, a musician named Nestor. On some nights he would entertain with the lyre and voice; occasionally he would join the actors on stage. His voice was fair, his lyre-strumming excellent. Yet he had not in all these months dared to speak to Gygax. The King of Tharta was not to be bothered with anything; he had servants and stewards for that.

"I know I am risking much," said Nestor. "But I was in Bat Zor's chamber… she is growing death's head mushrooms. She is planning some assassination. Thelema…"

"Get out," Gygax growled. "Get out now!"

Nestor turned and ran.

Gygax sat on the bench and took in the warm sunlight. He picked a blossom from a queen-of-the-evening and tore off, one by one, its dark purple petals. He breathed in its refreshing, sweet scent. Then he buried his head in his hands, and he wept.

THE ROYAL CHAMBER, THARTAN PALACE

Gygax had invited Thelema into his bedchamber to the exclusion of Zubeida. Even with that offer, she had refused. A dark hatred now burned within her, a deep anger that refused to relent.

In his nightclothes, wrapped in sheets of Khazidean linen, beautiful Thelema's words echoed through his mind—"An Eloesian man has but one wife, whom he loves and adores, and by whom he raises his children…" "You are not the man I thought you were… you are a southron tyrant." "May Amara strike you dead, and your barbarian southron gods!"

Her beautiful face would haunt him, reflected in the wan moonlight. Her locks of red hair would fill him with regret. Surely, her father Myno had heard of her ill treatment. Would Gygax have to repay her dowry? Surely, Thelema would not divorce the greatest man in Eloesus, wealthy and powerful beyond compare. Surely she would have better judgment than that.

Whom could he trust? Surely not Zubeida. Surely not Bat Zor. Only sweet Thelema.

Perhaps, he should run away. Perhaps, he should flee on horseback and ride into the Themurian wilds. He could become a devotee of Brecko, god of pleasure and wine—dress himself in rough panther-hides and work himself into a drunken frenzy. What would Bat Zor do then? She could do nothing but sit and stew. How would that wizened old witch deal with failure? How would she deal with an utter lack of control?

It struck him then—an idea rising like the glorious sun in dawn. As King of Tharta, he could call for the Pan-Eloesian Games. The games had not convened for more than a decade. Feats of strength and competitions that were meant to bring the city-states together—those, he would use as his escape.

He would have an excuse to leave the palace altogether. He would be free of Bat Zor and Zubeida and Thelema and the vizier. Yes, this could work. He would be free of the worries and the despair that ate away at him and chipped away his happiness.

In the far-away wilds of Themuria, in view of the Mount of Prophecy, he would hold the Games—and he would not return home for months. The people would be distracted; yes, yes, he would call for the Games. In view of the sacred mount, the troubles of the palace would stay behind him. They would be as far from him as the stars were from the earth. He would be free from the control of Bat Zor and her dark manipulations. He would be free from the competition of Zubeida and Thelema. He would, at last, have peace.

CITY PRISON, THÉNAI

How had the Mysterium allowed this to happen? How had Quartillo himself allowed it to happen?

As a young child, Quartillo had been set aside by the Master. He, the child of a sacred prostitute of Isdar, had been the one of the poorest and most disadvantaged of all the youth in the Potter's District. His mother Kosmeh had named him *Qartillach*—he had changed it, in his adolescence, to the more easily-pronounced Quartillo. Kosmeh had barely cared for him. By the time he had turned ten, she had died. An angry client had beaten her to death. The next year, the temple was closed.

Yet the Mysterium had replaced his family. Quartillo had loved his mother, and still did; yet the Mysterium was who fed him and all the urchins of the Potters' District. The Mysterium had never let him down—until now. Somehow, the king—no, "archon," of Thénai had seen through his disguise. Was this Theron a hero, or a god, or something even more? Or had Quartillo simply proven inadequate?

In the dingy prison, bound in shackles, Quartillo wept. Surely, this god Theron would not believe him. He would pay Quartillo's warning no mind. Fharas would come and conquer. No would expect them.

Who could believe *Qartillach*—the son of a whore and some unknown father? Gods rest sweet Kosmeh's soul.

OUTSIDE BACTRIS, KORTHICA

Theron had traveled the baking hot plains of Kersica and seen towns and cities suffering heavily under an oppressive yoke. He had seen Elehoi, chained and collared, slaving over fields of wheat, cattle farms and vineyards. He had seen mangy dogs sheltering in the hot sun. There had been squalor such as should never be seen in Eloesus. These Elehoi were a people suffering under the reign of slavers. It seemed the very earth groaned under the burden. Surely death was better than this—yet even death was denied them.

The road had crossed a bridge and now wound its way to the walls of a city—or what once had been walls. Kersepolan hoplites in red capes were heaving off the stones one by one—a typical tactic—revealing the mudbrick homes and winding streets within. Now, defenseless against their new masters, the conquered city of Bactris would be swallowed up into the Kersepolan kingdom. Its people, once citizens, would be reduced to Elehoi—the worst fate imaginable. Little by little their bodies would be worn down through onerous labor. They would cry out but never be heard. They would live hard, short lives in the baking hot sun; then they would vanish out of memory. They would return to the dust and not even the grand monuments they had built would remember them.

How can I ask the help of a people so brutal? Theron couldn't question himself now. The goddess Amara would be the judge of his efforts. He rode on into the midst of danger. The coward King Sardio had denied his request; perhaps Kyrion would prove different.

He found the king in the city square. Statues, surrounding a marble fountain, had been beheaded. Perhaps they had honored a god or hero greater than King Kyrion. Whoever those statues had honored would surely be forgotten, just as the slaves of Bactris would be.

"Who is this," said Kyrion, "who comes riding so boldly? And wearing a chiton no less. A Bactran? I'll put you to the salt mines." He was younger than Sardio, stronger-looking. He wore the heavy iron helmet with a sideways horsehair crest—as well as the thick bronze breastplate—with ease. No doubt he would be a formidable force on the battlefield, as skilled and brave as any of his men.

"I would not speak so rudely," Theron dared to say.

Kyrion growled and beat his sword against his heavy wooden shield. He stepped forward, as if to cut Theron down, horse and rider alike.

"I am the Archon of Thénai," said Theron.

"The leader of Thénai!" Kyrion laughed. "A city of peace-lovers. Artists, cowards, drunkards. Why should I fear the leader of Thénai? Tell me!"

"You should not be afraid of me," Theron said. "There is something you *should* be afraid of, though."

"There is nothing I fear," Kyrion answered. "Not even death."

Yet Theron could see the truth in his eyes—what Kyrion feared above all was what he inflicted on others. He feared becoming a slave, of becoming an Elehoi, of being put to forced labor in the salt mines and iron mines. He feared being shackled. Theron would play that to his advantage. "Fharas is coming," said Theron. "An army whose size the world has never seen and will never see again. An army of many hundreds of thousands… even a million. An army that will shake the mountains when it marches by.

They are coming to make us all slaves. Will you fight, Kyrion? Will you fight? Or will you make plans to surrender, like your friend Sardio?"

Kyrion did not want to voice the cowardice in his heart, which was written on his timid eyes and paling face.

"Will you commit to fight, together with Thénai and the other cities?" Theron asked.

Kyrion masked his fear with rage. "Go! Get out!" Anger was better than cowardice. "Leave me at once!"

Behind that anger was fear—fear not just of Fharas and its coming army, but of being seen as a coward.

"Goodbye, coward!" Theron shouted and rode away to sounds of "Get him!" and "Kill him!"

THE PALACE, THARTA

In the springtime, the trees were blooming and the grass was green. Here, in the garden courtyard, the quick Thartan winter had melted away into clear blue skies and a warm sun. The myrtle tree which lent the garden shade had donned its spring wardrobe—bright red blooming flowers. Nearby, lilacs filled the air with their unearthly fragrance. All seemed well in this private paradise. In just weeks, King Gygax would depart for the Pan-Eloesian Games—which he had announced just recently. He would no longer deal with the stresses and battles of the palace: the competition between Zubeida and Thelema, the controlling efforts of the vizier and Bat Zor. Instead he would endure the divisions and open enmities, the wrath and the anger of Eloesian cities. What was war and civilizational conflict compared to the strife of home?

The vizier appeared, the one who called himself Khusruh. The tall, hulking figure stooped as he made his way through the pointed arches. Once, he had told King Gygax of his origins. He had said his people were called the Khand, and they had fled disaster in their island homeland. They had often been viewed as the least of the Fharese peoples, yet they had proven their worth again and again—in war, in strategy, in governing. Their eyes had a tint of gold to them.

"What do you want?" said Gygax.

"I have good news," the vizier said. He wore, as always, the tiered golden headdress and rich robes of purple. "The Games—"

"How did you know about them?" asked Gygax, instantly realizing the stupidity of his question. How could he expect something that was announced to the public in Tharta and elsewhere to be kept hidden—even if he had not personally told the vizier?

"I have my ways," the vizier answered, and smiled. "I

would have recommended you stay home. You know I do not like those large gatherings—ripe for conspiracies and rebellions. But I also know you will not listen to reason."

"You're right," Gygax said.

"I feared Bat Zor would be enraged," the vizier said, "but in fact, she was intrigued. She has decided to accompany you to the Games. So have I. Our entire party will be traveling with you, Gygax… Zubeida, the baby and all."

Gygax's heart sank. He could not believe it. How could the gods be so cruel? How could he be so cursed? He gave a faint, false smile.

"I have not seen the Eloesian countryside," the vizier said. "I will make records for the King of Kings' reading. We shall all enjoy the Games, together."

Gods help me… I will never be rid of them.

THE LION'S GATE, THÉNAI

The journey back home, one which took many days, had worn down not just Theron's body but also his spirit. His thoughts had run rampant, on the road alone. He had never been so severely disappointed before—in his country, in his fellow Eloesians, but above all in himself. He had failed the Oracle and the Mount of Prophecy. His words could not convince the kings of Kersepoli, the most warlike city in the world—much less his home city Thénai, which he at last confessed was a den of soft philosophers and gutless cowards. *I have failed,* he thought as he rode through the Lion's Gate. "I have failed," he said aloud.

The streets were crowded with Thenoans going about their daily business—priests with their holy books, wives with bushels of fruit and pails of water, all ignorant of the danger that lurked on the horizon. The priests would be hanged, or perhaps burned alive as a sacrifice to Fharese gods. These humble wives, returning from the market, would be killed or forced to revere the fire god Athra, then enslaved and shackled in some harem. The jester, juggling knives on a street corner, would have his tongue cut out. The street urchins prowling the streets for pockets to pick would have their hands cut off in brutal southron fashion. The brothels would be closed and all shops and taverns would end business at dusk. The joy and love for living would become a memory, replaced with austere devotion to foreign gods and the constant fear of the King of Kings.

He wept for them as he rode. Tears trickled down his cheek, tasting of salt. He wiped them with his sleeve, not wanting to seem weak. Eloesus needed strength.

He made his way to toward the High City. Perhaps, he would resign and forsake his position as archon. Perhaps, that was best for Thénai. It was certainly best for him. He could not lead a nation of sheep. Fharas would swallow them up—but at least, if Eloesus had courage, they would die fighting.

"Theron! Theron!" a voice howled, filled with anger.

He looked down and saw, amid the crowd, a demiarch he recognized as Arko.

"Where have you been? You disappeared! Amara strike you dead, come with us at once!" he howled.

Grudgingly, Theron followed through the sea of people. He did not care what happened to the Assembly. As far as he could see, a Fharese spear through Arko's chest was well deserved—and the same for his two hundred friends. They had failed their duty to defend Thénai. They had failed their duty to be brave. They would try to negotiate terms of surrender which benefited themselves—but it was them, above all, who deserved death. Not the woman walking by, drawing water from the well. Not the children playing in the streets, or the piper seeking coin. They deserved to live.

~

These men do not deserve to live—he still thought that, seeing the demiarchs's faces. How could anyone support them? How could the people have voted for such cowards?

Hyron, Speaker of the Assembly, stood up and walked toward Theron. "My archon," he said. "You disappeared... irresponsibly! I have never seen such behavior in an archon—"

Theron wondered what would happen if he slashed hard with Pyrax. He wondered if the blood would flow in a trickle or if he'd bleed like a pig. He wondered if Hyron's head would come off easy, or if it would take a dozen slashes to pierce that fatty flesh. He was balding, with more gray hair than brown. There was a demented look to his face, to his bulging eyes.

A massacre in the Assembly! the town criers would declare. *The Archon has gone mad!*

Hyron took a step back, perhaps sensing the boiling wrath in Theron's eyes. His posture became demure. "The King of Thénai has announced the Games."

The Pan-Eloesian Games had not been called for years. Would Theron accompany them? Would he travel to Mount Hylea, to the sacred Mount of Prophecy, and watch the competition? Surely not, with the threat of Fharas looming above-head, with the dark and gloomy sky gathering storm clouds. Even in peace, would he ever take part with this nation of weaklings and cowards, this country of lechers and vagabonds?

"You expect to attend the Games?" asked Theron, showing his derision openly. "When the King of Kings has declared war on us? When he intends to take all Eloesus for himself?"

"It is tradition," said Hyron, glaring. "It is a national—no, a sacred, religious duty which the goddess Amara demands."

"Why don't you stay back?" asked Theron. "What if the King of Kings comes tomorrow? You'll be ready to fall prostrate and kiss his feet."

Hyron snarled.

"We will go!" howled Arko from the benches. "We will honor the goddess and our sacred duty."

"If the goddess is real, surely she has nothing but hatred for you." Theron turned and walked away.

"You have a prisoner waiting," Hyron managed to say as he left. "He is shackled in City Prison."

~

Finding himself strangely drawn to his duties, he made his way through the streets of Thénai, where a happy and prosperous people went about their business—young mothers with their children, merchants in their market stalls, pigs and goats, and dogs running wild. The red-roofed houses eventually peeled away before the batting waves and salty air of the sea.

The city prison lay close by the shore, an edifice of dark-colored stone. A high fence of pointed stakes surrounded it. At any time, it hosted several hundred prisoners. The Thenoans had abolished the penalty of death, according to their high-minded views. Where the Kersepolans hanged murderers and thieves, or chopped off their heads, the Thenoans would set them to weeks in prison with poor food and horrid lodgings to set them straight. Murderers would pay three-hundred *doukon* to the victim's family or be set to forced labor if they could not afford to pay.

The Thenoans took pride in this. But was that pride deserved? Was it more a sign of their weakness and lack of bravery? Theron sighed.

The guards let him by without a word. Into Thénai's City Prison he walked, into the dark corridors where wicked schemes and clever heists went to die.

He had known just who Hyron was talking about.

The Thartan who had duped him in the midst of the High City sat, cold and bound in iron manacles, in the dankness of the prison cell. He looked worse for the wear; his skin had taken on a pallid hue, and he looked hungry and perhaps a bit sick.

Yet when Theron approach, he looked up suddenly, an energy in his eyes. "I had a dream, Archon… a dream of a high mountain and a ruined temple. She told me—"

"Who is *she?*"

"*She* told me that if Phillipidēs fulfills his sacred duty, a mighty empire will fall."

He knew who this woman was. The Oracle of Hylea, who read the threads of destiny. She spoke of Theron as Phillipidēs, the greatest insult to the hero ever uttered. What was the sacred duty? And what was the mighty empire—Fharas, or their own?

"Warden!" Theron shouted and like a summoned ghost the warden appeared, fat and garbed in chainmail. "Set this man free. Give him the best meal you can and pay him thirty *doukon* for his troubles."

A look of wonderment came over the prisoner. "Thank you," he mouthed the words, but did not say them.

Theron turned and left. He had a creeping feeling of what his sacred duty was—but how could attending those useless games solve anything? How could it possibly stave off the ruin of Eloesus? How could anything stand in the way of the mighty Fharese Empire?

He racked his mind, trying to understand just how.

That night, he paced his room and walked into the cold night air, viewing the lights of the city below. He did not understand. He did not believe it.

Yet in time, he found himself packing his things into bedrolls and making preparations for the journey ahead. Who was he to question the wisdom of the Oracle? He had done his very best to understand her cryptic message, which she had so often uttered in dreams. Perhaps he did not have the right understanding, but how else could he make sense of it? The Oracle had commanded him to attend the Games, and to the Games he would go.

ROYAL THARTA GATE, THARTA

Heart full, with visions of the future dancing in his head, Quartillo passed through the Royal Tharta Gate—its immense archway carved with the images of the god Alabastros and the goddess Victrix—and entered his home. While he was entering, flocks of people were leaving by horseback and by carriage. King Gygax, he had heard, announced the Pan-Eloesian Games. Yet the poor people of Potters' District could never afford to travel so far, nor spend so much time away from their labors.

The white streets, fountains and bronze statues gradually faded away. The white stone road turned chipped and faded, then brown, and finally disappeared altogether, revealing the dirt beneath. The stone edifices and grand temples became mudbrick shanties and lean-tos. The air became stagnant and clogged with smoke and filth. Yet this smell, and this squalor, was Quartillo's home.

As a child, the son of a sacred prostitute, he had been ashamed of so much. He had been ashamed of his mother. He had been ashamed of the father he never knew. He had been ashamed of the Potters' District and all it entailed—the squalid living conditions, the sickly and unhealthy people wandering its streets—and he had been ashamed also of himself. He was ashamed no longer. Now, seeing the poor folk wandering the dirt roads, he beamed with pride.

He could no longer deny who he was. He could not wait to see Didyma and report his success to the Master.

Tonight, he would finish writing his play. Perhaps he would see it performed—maybe one day in the Seven Lions Theater. Fharas might invade and bring them fire and the sword... but for now, Quartillo was proud to be a Thartan. He was proud to be an Eloesian.

THE WORD OF IO

The priestess licked his open wound
Her eyes did shut, her lips did quake
Said she, "You shall have what you seek,
Fame imperishable and true
Yet long life shall not come to you
Nay, thirty years you'll never see
Nor twenty-five nor twenty-two
Life short and bitter, quick and dark
A candle burning quickly—yet
Fame imperishable and true…"

—Arkelaios

THE HIGH ROAD, OUTSIDE ARKADION

The road should have been familiar. Theron had passed it by in the company of Zoë and Phaido, gods rest his soul. He had traveled past Nautilos and Argon's Table like before—and yet it was different, now. The world seemed different. He himself was different. Back then, was it even possible to think that he might be Archon, the leader of Thénai? It was the furthest thing from his mind. Yet now he was leader of one of the world's great cities, a position undeserved and surely unearned.

The once-lonely road, crowded at all sides by pine trees and the vast wilderness, was now packed with people. In the frigid air the forest was still recovering from winter. Spring had arrived and the sweet smell of pollen filled the air, but patches of snow remained, clinging on after the severe winter.

Yet these people did not recognize him. They were from Tharta, Korthos and Kersepoli, yes—even Thénai—but even those from his home city did not recognize his face. He was as anonymous as he had ever been. He was not an archon but a fellow traveler. That was the point of the Games: all people were welcome. Rich and poor, farmer and city-dweller, Korthian and Thenoan, they were all Eloesian. It was one of the few glimpses of unity in a nation locked in bitterness and division.

Of late, some had questioned whether they were even of one kin at all. But Theron knew the truth; they had all come from one blood. They were all Eloesian—even if they did not see it. Their division and enmities would help the Fharese and ensure their total domination, but for now—during the Games—they were one.

Theron's horse was huffing as it made its way up a steep incline. The slope at last peaked, and there—towering in the distance—was the Mount of Prophecy. The small town of Arkadion lay tucked beneath its slopes. Its bent, jagged peak glowed in the sun. Its tip was covered in gleaming white snow. In the blue sky, in the cold air, Theron rode downward into the valley. The journey had lasted weeks and now his arrival loomed. He could not wait to rest his bones.

~

Past the timber houses of Arkadion, further on toward the Mount of Prophecy, the site of the Games appeared amidst the pines. It had been cleared—an area bereft of trees three miles in length and width. Construction had begun of makeshift seats and stadiums. The Games would not begin in earnest until the first day of summer—a month away.

After stabling his horse, Theron made his way to the cluster of tents where the Thenoans were camped. There Hyron, looking weary from travel, greeted him.

"The King of Tharta is having a feast tonight," he said. He looked down and frowned. "The Archon of Korthos and the Kings of Kersepoli will be there. I am afraid I am not invited."

Theron wanted to smile but he had begun to feel a bit of pity for the old man. All the bottled-up animosity faded at the sight of his glum expression. "I am sure they meant nothing by it," he said.

The frown faded; the sadness vanished from his eyes. Hyron glared openly at Theron, his archon, his leader. "Don't make a mess of things," he said. "No talk of unity or alliances, or Fharas."

Theron grated his teeth. The hatred for Hyron returned in an instant. Surely, the Assembly had already drafted their letter to the King of Kings. They had outlined the terms of surrender—"We will remain in power," it would say, surely, "you may kill our archon and replace him with a man of your own…"

~

Exhausted, Theron somehow managed to dress himself in a fine chiton and make his way to the Thartan king's tent. It was as tall as the House of the Archon in Thénai, and twice as wide, with multiple entrances to its living area. The sound of shouting voices and music echoed into the night from within. Before he reached the open tent-flap panic seized him; he remembered how inept he felt, how inappropriate the honor of archon seemed, how utterly un-statesmanlike he was. Then he sucked in a deep breath and walked in.

King Gygax was standing near the entrance, a handsome man with wavy brown hair. On his head was a golden sunray crown. He wore robes of purple silk, studded along the hem with white diamonds and blue sapphires. The fabric was decorated with suns, moons, stars, planets and all the celestial bodies—imprinted in glittering gold. A robe like that might be worth all Thénai put together.

By his side was a woman dressed all in black. Her entire body was covered in the plain garment, all save her beautiful olive-skinned face. Her lips were luscious and inviting, her eyes brown and nymphlike. This was a southron for certain. It seemed King Gygax had stricken a grand bargain with the King of Kings. Her stomach was swollen with child. In her hand was a plain cup of water—the southrons had many strange religions and beliefs. Had she foresworn all wine for the sake of her god?

The two were speaking with the kings of Kersepoli, Sardio and Kyrion, both dressed—as always—in bronze breastplates and flowing scarlet capes. In their hand were gold, jewel-encrusted goblets of wine. They both sported black beards and spoke in their gruff Kersepolan dialect.

I do not belong here. I was a common citizen before I became archon. I do not belong here at all.

In the distance was the Archon of Korthos, whom Theron—despite his tenure as leader of Thénai—had not yet chanced to meet. He was old, with silver hair, and wore a chiton like Theron. He was speaking to a group of other chiton-wearing men—a few demiarchs Theron recognized, but also others, perhaps archons of lesser towns and cities.

Two people were approaching. Like a distrusting sheep, Theron backed away before catching himself. Two people greeted him—one monstrously tall and the other short. The tall one wore a strange headdress—a three-tiered crown of gold—and had a face as dark as the night. His eyes were bright and luminous. Flashes of yellow teeth greeted Theron as he said, "You must be the Archon of Thénai. I have not yet been honored with your acquaintance."

"I am Theron," he said brusquely. The short person adjacent was a woman, garbed in black like Gygax's wife. All the soft-faced beauty of her compatriot was totally absent in this one— her complexion was wrinkled and aged, and a large, dark mole was near her mouth. As he looked upon her he could not help but remember the ancient tales of night hags—wicked old women who could kill by their ugliness. There was a gleam in her dark eyes, a pale light. Theron wondered if she was a sorceress, if she had the ability to turn him into a chicken or a goat. *I should not insult her,* he quickly determined.

"I am the vizier of the empire," said the dark-skinned man. "My name is Khusruh, but you may just call me Vizier."

"Well met, Vizier," said Theron. He felt so uncomfortable in these people's presence. King Gygax had invited these people into his life, into Eloesus's life—never knowing these were snakes and poison adders. At every step they were plotting. They were gathering information for the coming invasion, sowing the seeds of defeat. The Kings of Kersepoli knew. He wondered what went on in the minds of those warriors.

"And I am Bat Zor," said the woman.

Theron glanced into her eyes, though he did not want to. As he stared the ghostly light seemed to intensify and shine brighter. He saw treachery and plotting in those eyes. The ghostly light seemed to suck him in. The light grew brighter and brighter. Theron drew in a cold breath. Soon her eyes were blazing. He took a step back—and fell.

~

When he came to, the partygoers were crowded around him. King Gygax was poking him. The vizier looked confused. The kings of Kersepoli had looks of annoyance. Bat Zor had a thin smile on her face.

"My archon," said Hyron, pushing his way through the crowd, "you must get some rest."

~

When he returned to his tent, Theron began to piece together the vision he had seen while unconscious. He had seen, many decades ago, a band of Eloesians with swords and spears overcome a Fharese army ten times its size. The battle had taken place not in Eloesus but in one of the faraway colonies nearby a desert. He had seen Fharese horsemen and footsoldiers, armored elephants and war tigers overcome by a band of five-hundred Eloesians. He had seen a woman—Bat Zor—humiliated and infuriated beyond all reason. He had seen, in Bat Zor's heart, a deep, burning anger for Eloesus—an obsessive hatred which consumed her and drove her entire life. She masked this burning anger like the best of actors, never letting it rise above the surface. But the hatred was there, and it consumed her; it ruled her life. Everything she did, every plan she made, every word she uttered, every breath she took, was motivated by this hatred—to bring Eloesus down and crush it, to see its cities depopulated and its young people sold in the slave markets of the Far South. Hatred ruled her.

Theron made his bed and sat there in the cold night, listening to the crickets chirp. How could Eloesus stand before such hatred? When the most powerful empire the world had yet seen despised Eloesus, how could it remain? How? There was only one person to turn to, only one person he trusted. She read and wove the threads of fate; all knowledge was given to her, all knowledge and all truth.

MOUNT HYLEA

The road to the temple was long and winding, and the bitter cold wind pierced through Theron's cloak. His horse huffed and puffed furiously, breathing fog in the icy air. Soon springtime faded away and the upper portion of the peak—filled with pines sheer cliff faces—was covered with white new-fallen snow. Theron thought of turning back, but how else could he gain the answers he sought? How else would he know what to do? The oracle would tell him how to convince the leaders of Eloesus to fight Fharas—in the very presence of its vizier and first wife.

As he rode by in the wintry forest, a lynx appeared, snarling and batting its paw into the snow. Its brother, the lion, was gone from Eloesus, but these creatures remained. He wondered what it was thinking, whether—with its gleaming eyes—it could see Theron for the fraud and failure he was.

He passed the lynx by, and it did not follow.

~

Shivering and numb from the cold, Theron at last reached the temple, within easy view of the summit. He hopped off his horse. The temple's shattered and fallen pillars were covered in snow. Yet drums were pounding, spectral drums which echoed through the clearing. The drums were hard to resist—they invited dancing and ecstasy. In olden days, the prophetess would drink bottle after bottle of wine. Drunk and driven mad, she would utter prophecies with each breath, revealing all that lay ahead. The satyrs—her goat-legged attendants—would join her in her revels. One after another they would lie with her, yet she would never grow pregnant. They were creatures of another world; they could not conceive with human women.

How do I know this? He had read no books on the sacred oracle. She had been all but forgotten.

The oracle appeared, stark naked, running out from the temple like a wild animal. Her snake was twined around her leg, hiding her feminine parts. Her breasts dangled free. Her hair was wild and matted. Save her dark skin, she looked nothing like Zoë. Theron's old friend had been completely transformed.

"You know all this because you were there!" the oracle howled. She was drawing near, sprinting forward like a wildcat. "You were there in the ancient age, Phillipidēs… bit by bit your memory returns."

Theron still did not believe it. How could he, weak and ineffectual, be anything close to Eloesus' ancient hero? Yet he did have a memory of the oracle, and it grew clearer upon thought—a harem of satyrs attending to her every whim, torches burning in the summer night, debauchery and wine giving birth to prophecy and truth. He remembered the temple, but in his memory it was standing tall—with no pillar cracked or fallen. Its enormous roof overlooked the meadow in that ancient day, with a brightly-painted frieze running along its length—images of nude gods and goddesses and chiton-clad Eloesians bringing offerings to them.

"Why have you come?" the oracle howled. She was within striking distance. Her white, sightless eyes were mad. "Do not tell me, wicked one! I know all! Do not presume to tell me. You want guidance! Ha! Guidance! I will give you none."

"Then Eloesus is done for…"

The oracle bared her teeth. She never looked more like a wild animal than she did now. "Give up, then! And see the cities burn. The witch Bat Zor will have no mercy. She will see to it that every last building is torn down, every temple demolished brick by brick… only this temple on the sacred mount will remain. She will leave me alive… she will seek my counsel. I, the Oracle, will turn to

Fharas and spit on the memory of Eloesus."

Did the oracle bleed? If Theron removed her head, would she remain alive? Her callous and faithless words made him want to put it to the test.

"One word I give to you, one saying trustworthy and true… 'When the multitude gathers, you must make your move.'" She jerked and began to dance at the sound of drums. She was lifted a foot into the air. Twisting and dancing, she shouted nonsense words. Then she barked and roared like a lion, and screamed, "Go, before I devour your flesh!"

Frightened, Theron rode off. He had never been more disappointed. His fellow Eloesians were cowards and fools; now, even the oracle was faithless. Could her mad words be trusted?

Defeated and in despair, Theron rode deep into the night. Dawn was just hours away when he went to bed.

~

Over the next days and weeks, the empty field surrounded by tents began to transform. Benches were built of stone and wood. Cleared grasses became arenas and makeshift stadiums. As more and more people arrived from lowland Eloesus, merchant's stalls began to pop up, selling salted and cured meats, cheeses and, of course, copious bottles of wine. Wrestlers practiced their sport in the field; hopeful athletes tossed discuses and leapt long distances.

Near the tents, a great work was underway: towering bleachers which—when completed—would hold tens of thousands of Eloesians. Here, the main events would be held, and at the end of the Games, the victors would receive their laurel wreaths.

One crisp morning, as he was surveying the work, he sensed someone behind him. A large hand touched his shoulder and he bristled at the contact. The deep voice booming identified him unequivocally as the vizier: "Theron."

The vizier and the supposed "witch" Bat Zor were his enemies. Did he want to let them know that? It seemed the honorable thing to do. Yet he had to be deceptive, to cloak his hatred in polite talk and kind expressions. It was against his nature.

"Thénai is one of the great cities of Eloesus, I have heard," the vizier said.

Theron edged away from his touch. "If you ask a Thenoan, it is the greatest."

"Your petty rivalries amuse me," the vizier said. "One says 'Thénai is the greatest.' Another 'Korthos is the greatest.' Yet who can outshine the glory of the King of Kings and his empire?"

Always scheming, Theron thought. *Always making plans. He does not know that I know.*

"Thénai, it is said, has the best navy in the world. That it is something to be proud of, no?" The vizier laughed. "None of your Eloesian brothers can match your ships."

So proud, so boastful. He is saying the dhows of the Fharese would wreck them.

"Ships can bring goods and wealth from afar," continued the vizier, "but men live and breathe on land. They cannot leave it for long—in the air they will fall to the earth, in the water they will drown. Great kingdoms and empires are made on the earth, where man lives."

"Thénai and Eloesus have an empire of mind," said Theron. "An empire of ideas."

The vizier laughed and turned to face him, staring at Theron amusedly with his bright, almost gold-colored eyes. "An empire of ideas. You make me laugh, young archon."

"It is true," sneered Theron. "When has a Fharese lord written a great play, or made some wondrous invention? You people only destroy… you conquer lands better than yourselves and steal their wealth."

All humor, all smiles and laughter vanished in an instant. The vizier's glare was dark and stormy. "One day you will regret those words… you will lie prostrate before the King of Kings and kiss his feet."

Many things Theron was uncertain of, but one was beyond all doubt—he would never so much as bow before the King of Kings. He would die before that happened. *And die I will.* He turned and left, sensing the vizier's boiling rage even without looking. From now on, he would be considered an enemy. All politeness and protocol was gone. Eloesus, the vizier scorned and laughed at; but Theron he hated. Who else would so openly and proudly defy the King of Kings? Who else had such self-respect—and recklessness?

GAME GROUNDS

A week into the games, and the once-quiet field in view of Mount Hylea with booming with life. The shouts of the crowds in the stands were deafening as they cheered their favorite competitors. In front of the giant bleachers, footraces had gone on all day—men dressed in loin cloths, then women in loin cloths and brassieres, sprinted down the marked path. They were Korthians and Kersepolans, Thartans and Thenoans, Nautilans and Isteroi and Carchedonians—but in these Games they were all Eloesians. No nationality won an award for itself; only individual competitors—Eloesians all—could gain the laurel wreath crown. For just these few days, all Eloesians were united, immune to the bickering and small-minded quarrels that dominated the months and years to follow.

Theron left the bleachers, watching the runners sprinting down the course in their profuse sweat. There were darker things on his mind—like the oracle's words, that somehow the last hope for Eloesus lay here, amid these games and entertainments. How could it be?

He passed through the clogged paths, swarming with people. Stalls sold strips of salty pork and hunks of white cheese, wine by the bottle and by the glass, a southron delicacy called sherbet made of flavored snow, and much more. In these people, some laughing and some serious and austere, he could not help but notice a difference from the people who ruled them. The demiarchs in Thénai and Korthos, the kings in Kersepoli and Tharta—they all had such a different way of looking at life. They spoke with barbarian leaders such as the vizier and came to think like them; cooperation with the King of Kings was only natural—resisting him was madness. The common people despised all things southron— shepherds and city folk alike, they valued what little freedom they had. To those ruling over Eloesus' cities, their power and wealth was a given.

It struck Theron as he walked past the wrestlers, struggling on the dirt in view of a roaring crowd—the question of what motivated the cowardly demiarchs and the kings who dared not fight. Their lives were not in danger when they surrendered to Fharas; their power and safety would remain. The ruler of the Fharese Empire, after all, was a king over many kings—including, he would have it, Eloesus. Was it any wonder that the Assemblies in Thénai and Korthos were so willing to negotiate terms of surrender? They had nothing to lose… but these people, walking around Theron—mothers clutching infants, merchants and hoplites off duty—they had everything to lose.

Did Theron's hope lie in these people walking amongst them? But how could he convince them as a whole? How could he train these cobblers and fishmongers, these carpenters and stonemasons, to take up arms? Would they be willing to die? Would they even stand against the monstrous Fharese horde, or would they turn their backs and run? Surely, death and destruction would await them. Could Theron accept responsibility for such devastation and loss of life?

The wrestlers long gone, he came by the discus throwers. Three strong men, wearing nothing but loin cloths, were hurling the immense discs through the air. The sunlight gleamed along their metallic edges. He recalled the *solaricon* which Zoë had used to drive away the troglodytes. What would Zoë do? *Speak to me, Zoë.*

Yet Zoë was gone; she had shed her old self and become someone completely different. The new Zoë had told him what to do, in her own mystifying and impossible way. "When the multitude gathers, you must make your move." What move could he make? How could he possibly reverse course? The kings of Kersepoli, the assemblies of Korthos and Thénai, had already made their vote of disapproval.

He had not yet asked the King of Tharta, Gygax. Perhaps he—the pampered and arrogant ruler of Eloesus' greatest city— was his last hope.

~

Theron crossed the whole extent of the Games to find him—through crowd-clogged pathways where the swarms dodged mud puddles and stinking human waste, through fenced-in fields of equestrians practicing on their horses, past stick-fighters, past wrestlers both nude and clothed in the Thartan and Korthian styles, beside disease-ravaged beggars collecting spare *thalon* in their cups and beside wealthy nobles carried aloft in litters. At last, having scanned the Games' entire environs, he took a different tack, and made his way back to the tents.

The King of Tharta's tent was, by far, the largest of all the tents. It was twice the size of the House of the Archon back home. The thick smell of incense wafted from inside, combined with the aromatic herbs which were scattered across the rugs and beds within. In such a tent, surely even the King of Kings of Fharas would feel comfortable—it was a dwelling worthy of him.

Two guards stood at the door, bearing heavy spears. In Thartan style, they wore heavy breastplates and leather skirts. Full-face helms covered their faces, with blue horsehair crests. Their capes were similar to those of the Kersepolans, but instead of deep scarlet they were colored a rich blue.

They did not so much as flinch when Theron passed them by, entering through the tent flap. It appeared they recognized him, a visiting dignitary, a leader of the Thenoan state. *I am a man of importance,* Theron thought. *How did that happen?*

He found himself in a familiar scene. Lamps were burning, affixed to stakes, filling the grand entry room with dim light. Fharese rugs—purple and gold, woven in ornate designs—together with tigerskins and lionskins, completely covered the floor. Straw beds lined with soft Khazidean linen were interspersed throughout the room. Near one of the tent flaps, censers emitted smoke, filling the room with the thick scent.

Voices were echoing through the tent, loud and angry voices. Two women were engaged in a bitter dispute, one young, one old.

One shrill, howling voice Theron recognized unequivocally as Bat Zor. "You slut!" she howled. "You whore! These heathens have corrupted you."

"I am seventeen years old!" howled the voice of Zubeida. "I can make my own decisions! It's none of your concern if—"

"Keep talking! Yes, keep talking!" Bat Zor howled. "This heathen air has corrupted your mind, Zu. A little sip of wine may seem no great offense but it has already stained your soul. Your fathers' gods will no longer hear your prayers… Nawäl will curse you, Bel-Nohai will spit on you. In my day, a girl like you who sipped the devil's water would have her tongue cut out."

"I don't care!" howled Zubeida. "I don't care! I don't care! I hate you, Mother! I am wed to Gygax now and I'm having his child! One day you'll be gone! I love Gygax! I love this land… I love this country…"

A loud crack echoed through the tent. Bat Zor had clearly struck her. "Do not say that again," she began, "if you value your life." Controlled anger laced her voice. She spoke truly; Bat Zor would really kill her own daughter, her own offspring. "You are my child. In Shakrath, a daughter is no less than a slave. You are a slave to your mother until you marry a Shakrathite; then you are your husband's slave."

"I have a husband."

"Do not ruin our plans," said Bat Zor, "or I will make you rue the day of your birth. You will cry out for death but death will evade you. You will seek destruction but yet you will live. Do not question me. Do not disobey. You know what must be done. You know your father is coming. You know you must pave the way."

Zubeida cried out; apparently she was being restrained, whether by Bat Zor's hand or by her sorcery Theron did not know.

"Do not get in our way," said Bat Zor, controlled yet boiling rage filling her voice. "I will make you seek death… I will be worse than Mott himself."

Zubeida was sobbing now. "I hate you, Mother… I hate you…"

"I know," said Bat Zor calmly. "That does not bother me. All I care about is that you obey."

The sound of footsteps sent Theron into total panic. He ran toward the tent's exit flap—and was stopped by the appearance of Gygax.

The young king looked so much older than his thirty years would suggest. Bits of gray speckled his brown hair, and anxiety and worry lines had appeared on his once cherubic face. When his gaze met Theron's, he did not even feign interest. There was so much pain and worry in those brown eyes. He was not a man who enjoyed life… strange for the wealthiest and most privileged Eloesian there was.

"Could I speak with you?" asked Theron. "Privately."

Gygax said something gruff and unintelligible which sounded affirmative. He was leading Theron into a private room when Bat Zor appeared and behind her, Zubeida.

Theron gasped and clutched his heart. As he gazed upon that wizened face and met ever-so-briefly that cunning gaze, he could tell she knew everything. She knew he had been eavesdropping, she knew what he had heard. Already she had begun making contingency plans. Would she have Theron killed in the night? Would she set a poisonous viper in his tent or slip poison into his wine?

"Theron," Bat Zor said. "Archon of Thénai. A pleasure. I will leave you two alone." She walked away, making her way through the tent flap and then exiting altogether. Zubeida stood there, large with child. She hugged Gygax and he embraced her warmly.

"I hate her," she was murmuring. "I hate her so much."

"I know," Gygax cooed, stroking her back. "Go rest. You must take care of yourself... for the baby's sake."

"Yes, yes, the baby." She turned to walk away, revealing luscious dark eyes and soft olive skin. Tufts of silken black hair escaped from her black shawl. She was one of the most beautiful women Theron had ever seen.

Gygax, meeting Theron's gaze, was much less warm. He turned and led him into one of the tent's many sub-chambers, through an open tent flap.

Beds, perfumed with some aromatic plant, lay scattered throughout the spacious room. Gygax was almost glaring when he said, "What is it, Archon of Thénai?"

"I think you've been duped," Theron said.

"What?" Gygax said. "What are you talking about, *Thenoan*?"

He said the word Thenoan like a Kersepolan might say "Elehoi." "Fharas is intending to attack," he said. "They are intending to bring Eloesus into their empire... to enslave us all, to burn our cities and our temples, to pillage our fields, to take our children slave... to take our women captive."

When Gygax's dark, burning eyes met Theron's, filled with unspeakable anger, there was no doubt left: Gygax knew full well all the Fharese plans. Not only did he know full well, but he did not intend to stop them. Would he even collaborate with them? Would he even help them? "Get out!" Gygax howled. "Get out of here! Run!" He kicked Theron. "Get out before I have you killed!"

THE ROYAL TENT, GAME GROUNDS

As the Thenoan archon fled, Gygax's anger was replaced with burning shame. When he had agreed to marry Zubeida, he had known nothing of the King of Kings' intent. He had thought only of making a formal alliance, of combining—at the most intimate of levels—Fharese and Eloesian cultures. He had envisioned a fusion of the South and the East on a massive scale. He had never intended to be an accomplice to mass murder and destruction… he had never intended to bring about the end of Eloesus. Yet what choice did he have?

One night, Zubeida had covered their bed with white Khazidean linens and perfumed it with myrrh and cinnamon. She had removed her black *thawab*, revealing a thin smock of crimson-colored silk, which she had purchased at the clothier under the nose of her mother. Two things she had announced that night, before and after they made love: that she was pregnant and she was sure it was a boy; and that her father the King of Kings was calling up warriors from across the empire, a host of hundreds of thousands, and would capture Eloesus outright. Gygax he would leave in power but the other leaders he would kill.

Their son, he would name Gygax, though Zubeida wanted to name him Belshamon. And as for the coming conflict, Gygax would side with Fharas, and pray to every god in heaven that his throne would be preserved.

That did not stop his guilt, nor did it stop his fear. In ancient days, the King of Tharta would surely fight to his last breath. In the Megarine War, the King of Tharta Astromagos had personally led his armies into battle. Gygax was no Astromagos.

But Astromagos had not fought an empire as powerful as

Fharas. Astromagos had not fought a wise and cunning man like the King of Kings. Astromagos had fought a much less fearsome enemy: King Sosimon, who—as the tales told—was fat and gluttonous, besotted with women and always drunk on wine. There was no comparison. Gygax should not feel guilty; and yet he did.

He feared so much what was to come. He feared the King of Kings' control. He feared he would never be rid of Bat Zor and her entourage. He feared the vizier would never stop his meddling in everything. He questioned himself for a moment, wondering if that dark new world was worse than perishing in the resistance. Then he laughed at the absurd thought. Surrender was the only other option; and though the new era of Eloesian history might be dark and grim, he would weather it far better than most.

He pushed through the tent flap and found—to his horror—the vizier and Bat Zor, the two people in this world he dreaded the most. Bat Zor's dark eyes knew all. They knew when a lie was on Gygax's lips; they knew when he spoke any false thing.

"What was the Eloesian archon doing here?" said the vizier.

"He knows," Gygax said, not brave enough to lie and face Bat Zor's wrath. "He knows everything… he knows!"

GAME GROUNDS

Theron had never been so dour. He had failed somehow. There was no hope for Eloesus when all were so eager to surrender.

It had been days since his conversation with Gygax. The disappointment had not lessened; it had grown with each day. Now, as the Games came to a close and the winners were about to be crowned with laurel wreaths, despair had engulfed Theron's heart. He gazed at the bent peak of the Mount of Prophecy, at the white snow-capped peaks. He thought of the oracle's words, that—if he failed—she would join Fharas. She had offered no words of comfort, no words of advice except some cryptic message: "When the multitude gathers, you must make your move."

The people attending the Games remained ignorant of the coming disaster. They did not know that their leaders would abandon them to servitude. They did not know that the end of Eloesus was months away.

They do not know. "They do not know," he muttered.

Now the crowds were filtering into their seats, thousands upon thousands, tens of thousands upon tens of thousands, filling the giant pews, and then—when those were full—crowding around them. Theron, as an archon, had his own private box, but he would never share it with the people of the Assembly, a group which he had come to despise above all. There were no worse people in the world. Their cowardly mindset would drag Eloesus into defeat. Would they live on, humiliated, enslaved? Would Eloesus become a far-flung outpost of a dark and growing empire?

Theron ran. He did not know why. The naming of the winners was just an hour away. Still he ran. He ran from the coming disaster; he ran from Eloesus' certain end. Perhaps, he ran from himself.

THE STABLES, GAME GROUNDS

Theron entered into the stables. He was greeted with the pungent scent of horse dung, hay and earth… and a sight he did not want to see, a sight that enraged him beyond all else.

The vizier stood there. The hems of his royal purple robes were stained with dirt. His eyes, a strange shade of gold, glinted despite the dim illumination. His three-tiered golden headdress seemed dull and colorless without the sunlight. The robe and its patterned fabric, studded with sapphires and gems and rubies, seemed distinctly plain. Yet the arrogance and derision burned in his eyes greater than ever before. His true colors shone through; he despised Theron and considered him and all Eloesians lower than dirt. "Where are you going, archon?" he asked.

"That's none of your concern," Theron answered.

"Gygax told me you know our plans," the vizier said. "But neither you nor any of your fellow lowborns can do anything about it. Of all the human races you are the lowest. You will all be made servants. No more talk of this 'democracy' or foolish philosophy; no more talk of 'geography' or 'astronomy' or absurd pursuits. Gygax will be made the King of Kings' footstool. People such as yourself will be sold into bondage; you will work in the iron mines of Hittim or in the fields of some lord. You will be made lower than serfs. Perhaps you will be sold in the slave markets… some junk will take you to Cathay—gods know they are crueler masters than we."

He was trying to get to Theron, to anger him to the point of incoherence. He knew Theron could do nothing. He knew Theron wanted to resist, but couldn't have his way. He was lording this fact over him, teasing him, egging him on. "We will see,"

Theron answered simply, "one way or the other."

He would ride to the Mount of Prophecy once more. He would ask—no, beg—the Oracle for her advice. He would not leave until he had an answer—*what must I do?*

Theron ran to the stall and found it empty.

"Your horse…" the vizier said with mock concern. "It must have run away. How could that have happened? The stall door is open."

Theron drew Pyrax. "Do southrons bleed red? I will find out soon."

The vizier laughed. There was no fear in his eyes. "You would never. Your own people would kill you if you harmed a hair on my head. You Eloesians are always afraid. You are terrified of Fharas. You quake at any sight of my anger."

Theron drew in a deep breath. *I can't act rashly.* What would Phillipidēs do—Phillipidēs the wise, Phillipidēs the strong yet controlled.

"I am unarmed," said the vizier. "I have no dagger or saber to protect me. Go ahead. Prove my words wrong."

Theron shoved Pyrax into its sheath. "This is not over."

The vizier cackled as Theron walked away. "Run! Yes, run! It is as I said… you are a coward. You Eloesians are not men but dogs…"

~

"The champion wrestler," said the master of ceremonies, "is Amphidon of the city of Thénai…"

A heavily-muscled man walked up, girt in a loin cloth. Scratches covered his body where the other wrestlers had groped him. The master of ceremonies laid a laurel wreath on his head.

The people of Thénai, some in the stands in some in the

giant crowd surrounding the grounds, let out wild cheers. "Great is Thénai!" a chant broke out. "Great is Thénai!"

Theron still refused to join the cowardly Assembly in the private box. He had edged and pushed his way up to the front of the crowd.

Amphidon the wrestler, smiling at his victory, exited the grounds.

The multitude has gathered. What can I do? There was nothing to do but view his utter failure. Up in the private box, he could see the arrogant vizier taking his seat amongst King Gygax, his wife Zubeida, and his mother-in-law Bat Zor. He clenched his fists. *I should have killed him. I should have cut him to pieces.*

"The champion discus-thrower," announced the master of ceremonies, "is Vykno of the city of Arctos."

A pallid man with auburn hair—an Isteroi if Theron had ever seen one—walked up to receive his victor's crown. The laurel wreath was not of gold or silver, but winning at the Games was considered one of the greatest honors in the world.

In the stands, a group of several hundred Isteroi pounded their spears into the wooden seats. They were chanting: "Great is Arctos of the Isteroi! Great is Arctos of the Isteroi!" Some wore the beards typical of their kind while others—cognizant of current Eloesian fashions—were clean-shaven. They were all robust and red-haired, powerful warriors even as spectators.

Vykno left crowned with a laurel wreath. So many in Eloesus did not consider the Isteroi a part of their people, or even distantly related. Theron had once scoffed at the "barbarians," but no longer. They would all be tested together—Eloesians all. They would live together, they would die together. Fharas would stop at nothing to erase their name from the earth.

"The champion boxer," cried the master of ceremonies, "is Laocon of Korthos!"

"Great is Korthos!" a cry went out from the crowd. The faces were cheerful, even glowing. They were ignorant.

They are ignorant. The thought struck Theron harshly. He had not considered it before. *They do not know.*

"Great is Korthos! Great is Korthos!" the crowd cheered.

From the mass of people, a handsome youth appeared with curly brown hair and a well-muscled physique. Young women cheered as he approached and cheered even louder when the laurel wreath was set upon his head.

Theron found himself running into the open space, not knowing quite why. *To illuminate the ignorant. To let them know that their government has betrayed them.*

CENTER STADIUM, GAME GROUNDS

The master of ceremonies puzzled as Theron approached. The victor Laocon spared a curious glance as he disappeared into the crowd. Theron had no time for shame. He had no time for hesitation. There was no time for anything except to press ahead, to speak the truth, to illuminate the ignorant—to give a light to those in darkness.

"Go," said Theron, and the master of ceremonies obeyed.

Hundreds of glaring faces greeted Theron—thousands and tens of thousands—furious that he had interrupted their precious ceremony, that he had stopped their cities from being honored. In all this time, Tharta had not won a single contest; surely some athlete would take home the honor.

"Eloesians!" Theron cried. "Citizens! Free peoples of this great land… you have been betrayed!" Some of the glares faded, becoming interested, curious, perhaps alarmed. "Fharas and all its barbaric southron subjects are planning to invade! Their army has already left its moorings in Seshán!"

There were loud gasps. A few angry fists were raised.

"Your governments have sold you out!" cried Theron. "Korthos has made plans to acquiesce, together with its Assembly—never consulting the people. The Assembly in Thénai has made plans to surrender, against my will!"

Loud cries of anger echoed through the air. More angry fists were raised.

"The so-called brave kings of Kersepoli dare not resist! And Tharta is in league with the enemy…"

"Kill them!" some man howled.

"They plan to surrender! To throw away your freedom! To

sell you into bondage so that their wealth and governance can be preserved!" The faces in the stands were angry now, wrathful bordering on murderous. "I ask you, Eloesians," Theron continued, "free citizens and Elehoi, potters, sculptors, and servants, Korthian and Kersepolan and Thenoan and Thartan… even the Isteroi… what say you?"

"*Megali Eloesiou!*" a cry began. "Great is Eloesus" in the ancient tongue. "*Megali Eloesiou!*" The chant became deafening. In the Thartans' private box the vizier stood up in terror. Gygax had turned a shade of white. Yet his wife Zubeida had stood up and joined the cry: "*Megali Eloesiou! Megali Eloesiou!*" her mouth was moving with the crowd.

The vizier ran, together with the witch Bat Zor. The angry crowds would pursue him. They would find no rest and no shelter.

Eloesus had cast the die. Eloesus had made its decision. Eloesus would go to war.

CONTINUED IN BOOK 3, 'A PROPHECY'S END'

WE WILL RESIST

As Bat Zor and the vizier fled in panic, Gygax could not help but rage at his wife, chanting along with the crowd, *"Megali Eloesiou! Megali Eloesiou!"*

Then she suddenly stooped over. "It's happening," Zubeida whispered. "It's happening…"

Water had gathered on the floor.

What an inopportune time to have a baby. "Come on!" Gygax said, and grabbed her arm. "Come with me!"

~

In the morning, two things happened. Gygax heard word that the kings of Kersepoli and the Assemblies of Thénai and Korthos had acquiesced to the will of the people; they would go to war.

And a child was born, beautiful and healthy, male as Zubeida expected. He would be the next King of Tharta. Their peoples were forever unified: Fharese and Thartan. Fharseos they would call him, after the mythical ancestor of the Fharese race.

His wife's first words, as she nuzzled the infant to her breasts, were, "We will resist. We will fight my mother and my father. For us… and for Fharseos."

GLOSSARY

Thalos: A small silver coin, worth one-fourth a doukos. Plural thalon.

Doukos: The standard silver coin across Eloesus. It takes many forms but generally has the city's patron god cast onto the front and the victory laurel wreath on the back. Plural doukon. One doukos is about the daily wage of a skilled laborer.

Oros: A gold coin, worth fifty doukon. Plural orhon.

Talent: A unit of measurement, worth one-thousand doukon.

Alabastros: The king of the gods in the Eloesian pantheon. He is revered especially by the Thartans. As king of the gods, he is considered to preside over kingship, leadership, and royalty. He is often depicted as a wise old man. His favored animal is the lion.

Amara: The goddess of motherly love in the Eloesian pantheon. In Thénai and the Amazonian Isles, she is also the goddess of wisdom and battle. Although a mother, she is a virgin. Eloesian legend states she is the daughter of Alabastros and the Earth. Her brother is Tyros, god of war.

Amazons, the: A race of people living in the coastal islands off the Eloesian shore. Their women are far stronger and—some argue—more intelligent than their men. Though they look similar, amazons cannot breed with humans. The child of an amazon and a human is always stillborn.

Ansolon: The founder of the Thenoan democracy and perhaps all democracies. He led a popular revolt against the tyrant king and seized power over the government.

Arkadion: A village, the largest in the wilds of Themuria, called the Bride of the Wilderness. It is allied to Kersepoli.

Athra: In Fharese mythology, the god of fire.

Bactris: A city in Korthica.

Barbarian: A non-Eloesian. The Isteroi and the people of the Ten Cities are often considered barbarians.

Bel-Nohai: In Shakrath, the king of the gods. His name in Shakrathite means "Lord of the Sky."

Carchedon: A village in Kersica.

Cathay: A kingdom in the far east of Varda, barely known in Eloesus, considered impossibly distant and semi-mythical. The ruler of Cathay, called the Dragon Emperor, has established relations with the King of Kings in Fharas.

Chiton: A knee-length sleeveless shirt, once popular across Eloesus but now restricted to priests and government officials.

Elehoi: A large underclass, forming the majority of the population of Kersica. They are slaves, captives from Kersepoli's numerous wars, and all Eloesian by birth. The name means "little Eloesian" or "Eloesian-like."

Fharas: A vast empire, by far the strongest power in the world. It is ruled by the King of Kings, who is considered a living god. The word Fharas and Fharese also refers to a certain region and people—the heartland where the Empire began.

Fharseos: According to Eloesian myth and legend, Fharseos was the founder of the Fharese Empire. The legend states his father Menarchēs was the king of Megaris. A priest of the god Alabastros once refused to grovel before Menarchēs and in response, Menarchēs burned the priest alive, destroyed the Temple of Alabastros and slew all the god's followers. In response, Alabastros cursed Menarchēs with madness and caused him to fall in love with his sister. It was by this union that Fharseos was born. In his disgust at the situation, Menarchēs cast the infant away to die; but he was picked up by a bird and ferried south to the lands now called Fharas. There, he became a great hero, slaying the Fell Lion and the Serpent Queen. He founded the empire in the Fharese heartland and eventually achieved godhood; his figure was placed in the stars, where he forms the Fharseos constellation. This legend is hotly denied by the Fharese and those who hear it are provoked to wrath, especially about the incestuous union. They claim the founder of the empire was named Fhareedi, a just and moral man of high birth.

Harem: In Fharas, among the Great Lords and high-ranking officials, the separate living quarters for wives.

Hierophant: Sorcerers of lightning and thunder, as well as priests of the god Arephon. They mostly hail from Korthos.

High city: A common feature of all Eloesian cities, a towering high ground—natural or manmade—which serves as a fortress in times of trouble.

Himnaea: A famous poet from Tharta.

Hittim: A mountainous region in the east of Fharas, filled with productive mines.

Hoplite: The traditional soldier in the Eloesian army. Each hoplite has a helmet and a breastplate, a spear and a shortsword, in addition to an iron-rimmed wooden shield. When fighting, he locks shields with his fellow hoplites, forming an impenetrable wall as long as he holds formation.

Isdar: The goddess of fertility and carnal desire. She once had a large temple in Tharta, where sacred prostitutes were employed. This was shut down in the reign of the Fharaizing king, Gygax I.

Isteroi: See Isteros.

Isteros: A region in the north of Eloesus, along the river Ister. The Isteroi speak a dialect of Eloesian but are thought to be outsiders, due to their pallid complexions and frequently red hair. Arctos, the capital, is much smaller in size than other Eloesian cities.

Junk: A ship common to Cathay (see above).

Kalormenë: An isolated island belonging to the amazons.

Kersepoli: A large city, one of the four greatest in Eloesus. It is the most militaristic of the Eloesian cities and is ruled by two kings, either of whom may overrule the other.

Kersica: The region belonging to the city of Kersepoli.

Klytemna: A small village which once belonged to Korthos. The village and surrounding lands were seized by Kersepoli.

Khand: A group of people who settled on the shore of southern Fharas. They are known for their often gold-colored eyes and dark, almost black complexions. They have worked their way up in Fharese society and have become top government officials and bureaucrats. They say their home is not Fharas but on an island far out to sea.

Khazidea: A kingdom far west of Eloesus, heavy under the influence of Fharas.

Korthos: A large city, one of the four greatest in Eloesus. It is ruled by an Assembly, elected by the people, and an archon, elected by the Assembly.

Korthica: The lands belonging to Korthos.

Lion's Gate, the: The main gate of Thénai. Two lions are carved in stone above its giant double doors.

Magi: The priesthood of Fharas. They worship the god of fire, Athra, and revere all flames as sacred. Only youth with magical talent are chosen; they are taught both about the god Athra and also the skill of conjuring and controlling fire. Since magical talent is rare and can be found among the peasantry, becoming a magus is one of the few opportunities for advancement in Fharas's class-based society.

Megaris: A large city of Eloesus, the capital of the Ten Cities region.

Megarine War, the: An ancient conflict, shrouded in myth and legend, between the cities of Tharta and Megaris. According to ancient tales, the king of Megaris Sosimon fell in love with Prophylaia, the queen of Tharta. Sosimon abducted Prophylaia and the king of Tharta, Astromagos, declared war.

Monotheists: In Fharas, a sect that worships the fire god Athra to the exclusion of all others. The more extreme followers claim he is the only true god and is locked in a struggle with Shemesh, the lord of cold, night, and darkness.

Mott: In Shakrathite religion, a demon tasked with torturing those in the underworld.

Myno: The king of Isteros, called by some the Wolf King.

Nautilos: A city-state in the east of Eloesus, far removed from the ocean. Once great, its population has dwindled vastly and now it is more a village than a city.

Nawäl: A deity worshipped in Shakrath, presiding over goats. Devotees are called Nawlīm.

Nissos: A remote island off the coast of Eloesus, the center of the slave trade.

Old Dominion, the: A legendary empire which was said to rule the entire world. It was destroyed suddenly, in one night, by fire and ash. Its cities sank into the sea.

Phillipidēs: An Eloesian legendary hero, the son of a Thartan noble who fought in the Megarine War. According to myth, he was given a magic helmet by the goddess Amara which made him invincible to mortal weapons.

Potters' District: A section of Tharta, once home to potters but now merely a neighborhood of the extremely destitute.

Royal Quarter: A large section of Tharta, home to most of its monuments and temples. Only the very wealthy live there.

Saurians: According to legend, a race of lizard people which ruled a vast empire. They fed the people of surrounding civilizations to their god, a giant cobra. Stories state the amazons finally put an end to the legendary Serpent Empire and slew its god, burying the headless body deep underground.

Serfs: In Fharas, an underclass forming the majority of the population. They serve the nobility and are entitled only to a small portion of what they grow or earn.

Shakrath: A land in the east of the Fharese Kingdom, a harsh semi-desert region. The chief town is Umron, where the Shakrathite king also lives.

Slavery: The institution is widespread in Fharas and offers slaves no rights whatsoever; they are viewed as objects or tools, not human beings. In Eloesus, the institution is banned altogether in Thénai and heavily regulated in Korthica and Thartica. Slaves have no rights in Kersepoli.

Tharta: A great city, considered the chief in Eloesus. It is ruled by a king but has certain limited forms of democracy.

Thartica: The lands belonging to Tharta. The region allows for extensive irrigation which results in plentiful food.

Themuria: A region of Eloesus, wild and undeveloped. Being at a much higher altitude than the coast, snow is common in the winter. The region's chief town is Arkadion.

Thénai: A large city, one of the four greatest in Eloesus. It is ruled by an Assembly, elected by the people, and an archon, elected by the Assembly.

Thenoa: The lands belonging to Thénai.

Theurge: Magicians who commune with heaven (white theurges) or hell (black theurges). They summon helpers, often called archons—not to be confused with a city leader—who do their bidding. Black theurgy has been punishable by death for many years.

Tyros: The god of war. He is revered in Kersepoli; yet he is viewed as never favoring one city over the other, delighting only in battle itself and spilled blood. According to Eloesian legend, he was the son of Alabastros and the Earth. His sister is Amara and his daughter is Nix, whom he hates.

Victrix: The goddess of hearth and home, worshipped primarily in Tharta.

ABOUT THE AUTHOR

Cursed at birth with a wild imagination, Andrew Cooper spent his youth dreaming of worlds more exciting than Earth.

He is a graduate of the Odyssey Writing Workshop. His stories have appeared in Morpheus Tales, Fear and Trembling, Residential Aliens and Mindflights, among others.

CONTACT THE AUTHOR

Visit **www.aj-cooper.com** to sign up for the newsletter and stay up-to-date on new releases.

Find him on Facebook at:

www.facebook.com/AJCooperauthor

www.ingramcontent.com/pod-product-compliance
Lightning Source LLC
Chambersburg PA
CBHW031251210726
48287CB00003B/994